PRAISE FOR DRAGON VALLEY

"Dragon Valley is chock-full [illegible] t of epic battle thrown in. I work with young writers and see nuggets of literary gold all the time. But this kid, Luke Herzog, has unearthed a gold mine here. The writing here is a sparkling achievement." -- Kwame Alexander, author of *Acoustic Rooster and his Barnyard Band*

"It is rare to find such an imaginative, well written story from a first time author! When Albert Einstein said, 'Never stop thinking like a child,' this is what he meant!!"
-- Denise Brennan-Nelson, author of *Willow*

"What a treat! What an imagination! An epic story of scientifically-spawned dragons fighting to survive. Writing a novel isn't easy -- for Luke Herzog to write one before entering middle school is simply amazing!" -- Eric Elfman, author of *Almanac of the Gross, Disgusting & Totally Repulsive*

"Luke Herzog has written an epic dragon tale full of adventure and heart. An impressive story written by a clearly talented 11-year old kid!"
-- Robin Mellom, author of *Ditched and The Classroom*

"The image in Christopher Paolini's rear-view mirror is a fast approaching superstar to the genre of fantasy writing. Luke Herzog's debut novel *Dragon Valley* flies at breakneck pace as a new clutch of dragons struggle in their (timeless) quest of good versus evil. Sprinkled with symbolism, readers will love taking flight with this fresh cast of characters."
-- Mike Shoulders, author of *Say Daddy*!

"Luke Herzog is a great storyteller! Kids will love the colorful world he created in *Dragon Valley*. The book is quite an achievement - I look forward to more from this young author."
-- Christy Raedeke, author of the *Prophecy of Days* series

DRAGON VALLEY

LUKE HERZOG

You see things, and you say "Why?" But I dream things that never were, and I say "Why not?"
-- George Bernard Shaw

Why Not Books
www.whynotbooks.com
Pacific Grove, CA

Dragon Valley
www.dragon-valley.com

ISBN: 978-0-9849919-0-7

Printed in the United States of America
Library of Congress Control Number: 2012931489
April 2012
Second Edition

To my dad, who assisted me throughout the creation of this book and inspires me to be who I am.

To my mom, who always encourages me and is the one most responsible for figuring out the publishing process.

And to my brother, Jesse, who survived reading the first draft and who is my favorite (and only) sibling.

CONTENTS

THE FIRST AGE

THE SECOND AGE

THE THIRD AGE

THE FOURTH AGE

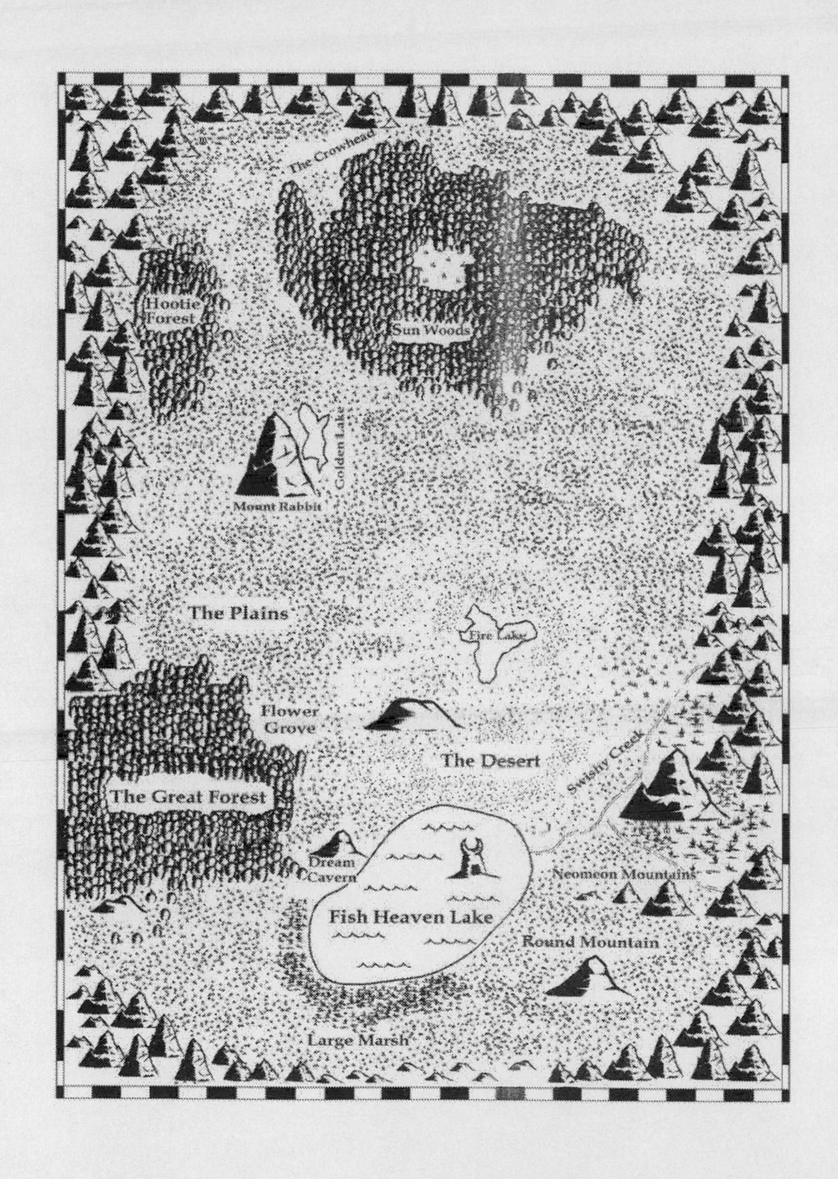

DRAGON VALLEY

PART 1:
THE FIRST AGE

1. BIRTH

The star orb filled with energy and glowed like the sun. The computer hummed. A blinding light flashed.

"It worked! It worked!" shouted Dr. Huffman with joy. He almost flew out of his seat.

Dr. Ray T. Huffman, Jr. was a busy man. His inventions had changed the world. He had discovered star energy, found the tenth planet and named it Vulcan after the Roman smith god (and "Star Trek"). He also discovered the fifth dimension. Then came an announcement in the holographic newspaper:

> Dr. Ray T. Huffman Jr. is at it again. He is about to reveal his latest remarkable invention. He won't say what it is exactly, but he did say it will be magical. Huffman said it is expected to be completed on July 25, 2043.

The date had arrived. It was time to make history. He pulled a big switch in the middle of the room. There was a flash of blinding light. Then, there, in front of his eyes, stood the first ever scientifically-spawned dragon. It was red, six inches long, and alive. A few minutes later, there were four more. The second was yellow, then blue, white and black. Black was different. The doctor didn't yet know. He named each of them by the color of their scaly skin.

"Red, Yellow, Blue, White and Black," he said. "You are dragons. Male dragons are drahs, and female dragons are drais. Sleep now, my children..."

* * *

The meteor that crashed in 2016 near Goose Lake in Northern California, where very few people lived, left a big valley, a perfect place for dragons to thrive. Dr. Huffman was on an airplane flying there. All five dragons were in a basket, and all five were sleeping. The sounds of her brothers and sisters snoring woke Yellow. She poked her head out of the basket. Where was she? What was that sound? Yellow looked around. She saw a familiar creature, the one who had told her and her brothers and sisters to sleep. She walked over to him.

"Wh-where are we?" she stuttered, afraid. "Who are you?" She was surprised that the words in her mind came out of her mouth. Dr. Huffman had bred them with great intelligence.

"Don't be scared," he said. "My name is Ray. Right now, we are flying in an airplane to a valley where you are going to live."

"What are you?" asked Yellow, gathering courage.

"I am a human. I made you from star energy – energy drawn from the stars," Ray explained.

"What are stars?" asked Yellow.

"Stars are lights in the sky. You can see them out the window."

Yellow looked. "Wow!" she said, but she was tired. And soon she fell asleep.

* * *

Blue woke up. What was that amazing smell? He ran to it as fast as he could, then he saw it. It was some sort of clear container, holding something that he strongly desired. Blue managed to unscrew the lid with his claws, and he took a sip of the liquid. It was cold. He loved the taste of it.

"So you like it?" said a voice behind Blue.

Blue turned around. It was the same creature who had told him his name.

"What are you? What is your name? Where are we? What is this I drank?" he asked. "Can I have more?"

"Not so fast. My name is Ray. I am a human. We are flying on an airplane to a valley where you are going to live. What you drank is called water. There will be lots of water at the valley. Also…"

But Blue fell back asleep.

* * *

Pink light awakened Red. She looked out the window and saw an amazing sunrise. Red put her claws against the window, staring in awe. Then suddenly, the airplane jolted, and Red flew from her seat.

"Aaahhh!" she shouted, feeling like she was falling. But then she wasn't. She heard nothing but the wind. Wait, that wasn't the wind. It was her wings. Red was flying within the flying machine.

* * *

"Wake up, Black! Look at the water!" yelled Blue.

They were on a boat, moving through the darkness.

"What's water?" murmured Black.

"You have to see the stars! They're so bright!" exclaimed Yellow.

"What are you talking about?" asked Black, who was now awake.

"I wonder what it is like to fly near those stars," said Red.

White just looked around, as if searching for something. He hadn't found it yet.

Ray stepped forward. "Dragons, come over here. It's time we talked."

Red, Yellow, Blue, White and Black moved toward him. "Where are you taking us?" asked White.

"A special valley," answered Ray.

"Where are we now? It has so much water," said Blue, looking quite thirsty.

"We are on a ferry boat on Goose Lake."

"What are we going to do when we get to the valley?" asked Red.

Ray looked at each of them. "I... am going to train you."

* * *

The dragons had begged Ray to tell them what he meant by that. Train them? But he said nothing else. So White had flopped down on the floor and had fallen asleep.

"White! White!" whispered Red.

"What is it?"

"We're at the valley!"

White shot up and almost tripped over his claws in excitement.

"Brothers…" murmured Red, shaking her head as the ship docked.

"We're here!" hollered Yellow.

"Where's the water?" asked Blue.

"Follow me," said Ray.

They walked through a little forest for a few minutes and then came to a grassy field next to a pond.

"WATER!" yelled Blue.

"You can go in the water later," said Ray. "Right now, we have to look around your new home."

Blue sighed. They walked along a dirt path into another, larger forest. They reached a clearing in the middle of the forest.

"You can sit down now," said Ray.

"Yes, finally!" said White. "I'm so hot. We should call this Sun Woods."

Ray cleared his throat. "First you must learn how to hunt."

How do we do that?" asked Yellow.

"Oh," said Ray, smiling, "I have no idea."

"You don't know?!" Yellow blurted out.

"Not at all," said Ray. "You do, though."

"What do you mean?" Black asked with a touch of annoyance in his voice. *That was Black's first question to Ray,* thought Yellow. *Why is he so grumpy?*

"Your instincts will tell you what you eat and how to eat it."

"Our what?" asked White.

"I'm sorry. Your instincts are when you think or want or are naturally good at something, and it's because you were born that way."

"How do we use it, though?" asked Yellow.

"You will know," said Ray.

White and Red, go north," commanded Ray. "Blue, you go south. Yellow and Black, go east."

The dragons didn't know why, but they knew which way to go. As Yellow and Black wandered through the forest, something darted from under a bush. Yellow ran to it, but Black was faster. He killed it quickly. Then he began to eat it.

"Can I have a piece?" asked Yellow.

"No, this one's mine," said Black with a smug look on his face.

"Alright," sighed Yellow. After Black devoured his food, they set off again. Yellow saw a flying animal and jumped for it, but it flew away. "Arrgh!" yelled Yellow. "I'll never catch anything."

"Hah! That's true!" teased Black.

They walked on. Suddenly, a hairy thing - the same kind of hairy thing that Black had caught before - darted from another bush. Yellow ran and pounced on it. Just then, Black grabbed it.

"That's mine!" screamed Yellow.

"Then fight for it." Black dropped the dead creature between them. They began to circle each other. Yellow jumped toward him, but he dodged her. She tried again, but he dodged again. Black's eyes narrowed. He jumped and pinned Yellow down. "Mine," he whispered. Black leaped off Yellow and ate the hairy creature. As they walked back to Ray, they didn't speak.

What a weak dragon! Black thought. *Every time we fight, I'll beat her.*

Finally, Yellow spoke. "I will get you, Black. I will get you."

"Never."

2. THE NAMING

As Yellow and Black were fighting, Blue was wandering around looking for food. Whatever he found didn't seem to taste good. He passed a lake and had to use all his willpower not to jump into it. He then came to a desert. He found no good food there either. Then Blue came to the biggest lake he had ever seen. *I have to jump in,* he thought. *I have to.*

He jumped.

"Aaaah... that's more like it," he said to himself. Blue felt cool and refreshed. Then he saw a silver creature darting through the water. He caught it and ate it. It was amazing! Blue grabbed more... and more... and more.

* * *

When will they come? Dr. Huffman was waiting for the dragons to return. *Now, where did I put my reading glasses? That was my fourth pair! Ah, here they are – the dragons, at least.*

"I got a big, fluffy animal!" exclaimed Red.

"And I got a small, slippery thing!" hollered White.

"Red, you found a sheep. And White, you found a snake," said Ray.

"I think I'm going to call it a *sler,*" said White.

"As you wish, White." At that moment, Ray saw Black and Yellow coming.

"I caught a fast creature!" bragged Black.

"A rabbit," Ray explained.

"What did you get, Yellow?" asked Red.

"Nothing."

Ray looked at Yellow with a curious expression.

"Where's Blue?" asked White.

"Mmmphh... Mmmphh." Blue came running up with his mouth full.

"And those," said Ray, "are fish."

"Now what do we do?" asked Blue, after he finished off the last of his fish.

"Now I will teach you to fly," said Ray. "Red has already learned this, but now the rest of you shall learn."

* * *

Red couldn't wait to show the other dragons how she could fly.

"This field looks like the head of a crow, a bird," said Ray.

"Let's call it the Crowhead," said White.

Ray smiled. "You can name everything here. This is your valley, dragons."

"Well, then let's call it Dragon Valley," said Yellow. "What now?"

"Move your wings up and down ten times," said Ray. "This is called pumping your wings."

When the dragons were on five pumps, Red was already in the air. Yellow, White and Blue gasped in amazement. Black just grunted.

A few seconds later, the rest of the dragons joined Red in the skies above Dragon Valley. Well, most of them.

"Why can't I fly?" asked Blue, still on the ground.

"You simply aren't built for it," Ray explained. "You're special in other ways. You're a swimmer, Blue. I could tell when you were born, and the first thing you sought was water."

Ray called to the flying dragons. "Now, I want you to race to that small redwood tree. Whoever is first gets a rock. Whoever finishes second gets a leaf. And whoever comes in third gets a twig. Ready? Get set… Go!"

Red felt the wind in her face. It was a great feeling to be in the skies, especially above Dragon Valley. She felt as if she was the only creature in the air, as if it belonged to her. She easily reached the redwood tree first and heard Ray's voice from far below.

"Red wins!"

* * *

Black couldn't believe it. *Red won, and I only came in third. I got a stupid twig, while she got a nice, smooth rock. Even Yellow beat me. And I only beat White because he has shorter wings.*

Yellow's voice came back to him: *I will get you, Black. I will get you.* A piercing roar snapped him from the thought.

"It's a mountain lion!" shouted Ray.

"Yes, fear me, human. Fear the mighty Darondo, leader of the Neomeons," yelled the mountain lion.

"What's he saying?! What's he saying?!" hollered Ray.

He had programmed the dragons so that he could speak with them. But somehow he sensed that the dragons could speak to other creatures, too. However, the dragons just stood there in shock.

"Why are you here, and who is your leader?" continued Darondo.

Red stepped forward. "I am Red. We have come here to seek homes. Our leader is this human, Ray Huffman."

"What kind of species are you?" asked Darondo.

"What?" asked Red.

Darondo could see that he was speaking to a young creature. "What kind of life form are you?"

"We are dragons. Why are you asking us this?"

"Because I have never seen your kind before. I would like to study you more closely."

"What is he saying?" Ray repeated.

Yellow filled him in. Then Ray thought for a moment before speaking to the dragons. "I am reluctant to train you in this, but you must learn to how to protect yourselves. I will teach you how to fight."

They walked south, the same way Blue had, past the first lake he had found. Darondo joined them. They named it Fire Lake because it was evening, and the sun reflected on it, making the water look red like flame. Then Ray began to explain how to fight.

"Slash with your front, right claw. Then slash with your front, left claw. Do this faster and faster, and you'll be doing the basic fighting movement."

After a few minutes of training, Ray added, "Now, do you want to try something harder?"

"Yes!" yelled Black.

"Well, try this... Stand on your back claws, jump and do a slash in the air. We'll call that a *jash*."

On Black's first try, he did it correctly. It took Red and Yellow two times and Blue and White three times. Darondo tried it, too. He couldn't quite jump the way dragons could.

"Now it's time for another contest," said Ray. "Blue will face White. Red will face Yellow. Whoever wins that will face each other, and whoever wins that will face Black. Let's begin."

Blue and White were first. Blue did a basic fighting movement, which White dodged. Then White did a jash, which Blue dodged. Next, Blue tried a jash, but fell down. White pinned him down.

Red barely won against Yellow. Then Red pinned White on his first attack. It was Red versus Black.

Red did a jash, but missed. *She can't get me,* thought Black. *This time, she won't win.* Black tried to jump on Red, but she dodged. Red did another jash, but couldn't pin Black down. This went on for several minutes. Finally, Black jumped in the air, turned three times, slashed and pinned Red down.

"Black wins!" shouted Ray.

* * *

After watching the fighting contest, Darondo left the dragons and told them he would come back to visit often. Yellow and the others followed Ray to a cave that Blue had seen while trying to hunt.

"I see it!" shouted Blue. Yellow smiled. Every time Blue talked, it reminded her of him talking with a mouthful of fish.

"Finally, I'm so tired," said White.

They walked into the cave. Yellow found a ledge covered in moss. She decided to call the moss *sofin* because it was soft and she liked to cuddle in it. She closed her eyes, but as she did so Ray ran in.

"Yellow! Yellow! Black's gone!"

3. SHADOW ISLAND

The night was getting darker and colder. The wind was getting faster. This was the weather Black liked. He felt a raindrop on his tail. Black looked up. Gray clouds were coming in. He was walking closer and closer to the lake. *What's that in the water?* He saw steppingstones. They led to something in the middle of the lake. Black jumped on the first one, then the second, then the third.

"Aaaaaaaaaaaah!" He slipped and fell into the lake.

* * *

"Ha! Ha! Ha! What a splash!" Vron, a vampire bat flew toward Black. "I haven't seen a splash that big since... since... since I lived with seagulls in the ocean. Yes, that was a splash, indeed!"

"What's a seagull?" asked Black. "What's an ocean?"

"Why, a seagull is a big, fat, white bird that dives for fish in the ocean, which is like this lake, but far bigger. Yessiree! Seagulls ain't nothing like bats!"

"You're a bat?" asked Black.

"Vampire bat, to be exact," said Vron. "Yes, better than those stinkin' cave bats."

"What's a vampire?" asked Black.

"You're funny as a fang, ain't ya. You sure do ask a bunch of them questions! Human-folks named us. We bats don't know what a vampire is. Why don't I follow you to the island."

"Island?"

"Yessiree! We bats call that little bit o' land Shadow Island. Some folk say it's haunted."

"Haunted?"

"Tell ya on the way… c'mon!"

* * *

White and the other dragons were on the search for Black. *Where would Black go?* White let his mind wander through his day. The mountain lions - or Neomeons, as they called themselves - had shown some impressive skills. *With their noses, they could smell Black out!* White ran to Ray and told him his idea.

"Brilliant!" exclaimed the doctor. "We shall set off immediately!"

* * *

Darondo looked down at the stormy valley from the top of Echo Mountain.

"Your grace, you should come inside. You should be protected from the storm," said Darondo's assistant, Bruoo, from behind him.

Darondo did not turn around to look at him. "A king does not need to be protected, but his subjects do. Are all Neomeons inside?"

"Yes, your grace."

"Stop calling me that!"

"Yes, your grace."

"Bruoo!"

"Sorry."

"Call a meeting in Mountain Hall," said the king.

"Of course, Darondo."

"Thank you, Bruoo. You may go."

Bruoo walked into a cave at the top of the mountain. Darondo stared at the valley for several moments and then walked into the cave, as well. He stood on the top of Leading Ledge. It reminded Darondo of his king ceremony. It had been three years since that had happened. Darondo looked down at his fellow Neomeons.

"Welcome one and all to this meeting. I have gathered you all tonight to speak about our new visitors."

Voices from the crowd rose up. "Who are they? What do they want?"

"They call themselves dragons. They have come here to seek homes. I don't know why, but I sense that they are good-hearted young creatures - mostly, at least. If anyone is to harm them, you will be..."

"Help! Help!" Red suddenly appeared. "Black is gone."

"They are here now!" exclaimed Darondo. "And it seems they need our assistance."

* * *

Black knew he could trust this bat. He just knew. They were walking on the steppingstones and getting closer to Shadow Island.

"So you said you would tell me why Shadow Island may be haunted," said Black.

"That I did. That I did," Vron replied. "Now, this ain't one of those ol' ghost stories..."

"Ghosts?"

"Yessiree! We bat-folk like to make up them stories."

"What's a ghost?"

"Them ghosts are spirits from the dead. There ain't no ghost-folk in this story. Yessiree! It all started on a stormy night like this one. An old stinkin' cave bat was flying over this here island when the trees on the island grabbed the old coot. They're called grabbin' trees. None of them other bats ever came to this here island again. Except for me! Yessiree! That's a load of mish-mash and gobbledygook!"

"Well," said Black, "here we are!"

"Yessiree! C'mon. Let's take a little look-see around!" Vron nearly yelled. "Sorry, I'm a big bit excited!"

* * *

"I'm sorry, but my clan has decided we cannot help you unless you give us something of use," explained Darondo. Yellow interpreted for Ray, who still could not understand the Neomeon language.

Ray is not as bad as I feared, Darondo thought to himself. *Ray is of good kind.*

"We could trade you sofin," said Yellow.

"Sofin?"

"It's a very soft moss that I found at the cave. We could be... sofin traders. Every time we need the Neomeons, we could offer you sofin."

"But, what use would we have for that?" asked Darondo.

"You could put your cubs in it! It would keep them warm."

"Hey, that's pretty good. I'll show you around the clan sometime," said Darondo. He gave a big Neomeon smile. "And... we will help."

* * *

Vron was overly excited. He was the first bat to visit the island since the old cave bat. Vron was flying next to Black, who had just found a cave in the side of a hill.

"Now this here is a cave." The moonlight made the cave glow nearly as bright as the moon itself.

"I'll call this place Moon Cave," stated Black.

"Well, then, what do we do now?" asked Vron.

"We explore more, of course."

* * *

Darondo signaled his clan to stop. The scent trail had stopped at the third steppingstone. *It seems like he fell into the lake. He probably climbed back on and went to the island... or drowned*. He reported this to the dragons.

"Let's go to the island, then," said Blue.

* * *

"Now, these here are the grabbin' trees," said Vron, pointing his wing at a few ghostly trees with absolutely no leaves.

"I don't think we should go near them," said Black, sounding a little frightened.

"Same with me. Yessiree!"

They stood there for a moment. Then Vron said, "I gotta go! There be mountain lions comin'! I sense 'em!"

"Oh no!" yelled Black, as Vron flew away.

"Oh yes!" said Darondo from behind him a moment later.

Ray stepped up next to Darondo. "Black...." That was all he said.

The dragons walked slowly back to the original large cave that they had found. They named it Dream Cavern, but no one dreamed that night. In fact, they barely slept.

4. DIAMOND IN THE ROUGH

Yellow yawned. It was mid-morning. Ray had told them all to hunt alone. Then he asked them to come back because he had something important to tell them. At the moment, Yellow was chasing a very fast rabbit. She jumped on it and killed it with one swipe. Yellow ate it slowly, savoring its taste. *Finally, food*! Then she strolled back to the cave where Ray and the other four dragons were waiting. As the cave came in sight, she thought about what Darondo had said: *I'll show you around the clan sometime.*

When? Yellow was pondering this when she walked into Dream Cavern.

"Ah, Yellow. Good, now we're all here. There is something we need to talk about," Ray said. "You need territories."

"Territories?" asked Blue.

"Territories are where you live."

"But, don't we live here?" asked Yellow.

"Yes, but... You need certain places in this land. You see, when you get older... and look how old you're getting already! You're getting bigger and bigger every day! You will start to want certain places in the valley. Let's find them now, so when you're older you won't have to go through the trouble."

"So now what?" asked White.

"Split up, and each of you find a place where you think you might like to live. Then return."

* * *

Right away, Red thought of the desert. She walked back there to take a closer look at it. *Ah, the sand is so soft, and the air is so warm. I want to live here.* She hurried back to Ray.

* * *

Blue also knew straight away that he wanted the lake for his territory - the big lake, which he called Fish Heaven Lake. He ran to it and splashed in. *Yes, the lake is right for me. And it has so many fish!* He swam for a while beneath the mid-day sun, then ran back to Ray.

* * *

Heading north, White wandered past the home of the mountain lions. He started climbing a hill. As he got higher, he realized it was more than a hill. It was a mountain. White looked up. The sun was still high in the sky. It was early afternoon, but it was freezing. Snow was on the ground. He liked it, though. He would live here.

* * *

It was evening. Yellow was in a big forest. She heard the call of a brown bird - Hooo! Hooo! Hooo! Yellow named it a *hootie* because of its odd sound. She still had not found a territory. She thought about what Darondo said about showing her around his clan's home. Yellow was still wondering about this when she stepped out of the forest, and she was just able to see the sun set before it disappeared. She was standing on a soft, grassy field with beautiful pink flowers. This was it.

* * *

Midnight was a dark and cold time, but not for Black, who was on Shadow Island.

"So you are saying that we can meet with each other every night?" Black nodded. "Yessiree! That'll work!" shouted Vron.

The island was Black's territory.

* * *

Over the course of several days, the dragons learned many new things - like how to do a swirl in the air (which Red mastered), how to get two rabbits at once (which Yellow learned quickly) how to perform a *kodge* (which was when you dodge and then kick your opponent), and how to do a *pait* (which is when your opponent jumps at you and you hold out a claw for them to fall on) and a *back-kick* (which is exactly what it sounds like). All of these Black was able to do on his first try.

* * *

"Yellow! Yellow!" shouted Darondo.

Yellow was doing battle training and practicing her kodge when she heard him calling.

"Darondo! Finally!" she hollered.

Darondo asked Ray (with Yellow translating) if he could take her to the Neomeons' mountains. Ray agreed. As Darondo and Yellow began walking, Darondo said, "Call me Dar. My friends call me that."

"I'm your friend?" asked Yellow.

"Of course you are! With that moss… you saved an important cub!"

"I did?"

"I will tell you about it when we get to the mountains. Did you know that the tallest mountain of our home territory is called Echo Mountain? And the second tallest is… "

He talked until they reached the mountains. There was quite a bit of commotion when they arrived.

"Your grace, you are here!" said Bruoo.

"You know not to call me that," said Darondo, looking slightly embarrassed.

"Of course, Darondo. Especially today."

"Would you like a snack, your majesty?" asked another mountain lion.

"No, but I bet my friend would," answered Darondo. "Come to my den, Yellow. It's nice and comfortable." They walked to a den that seemed small for a king. Yellow heard squealing sounds from the den next door.

"What's that?" asked Yellow.

"I'll tell you inside. Melendi will come with a snack."

Yellow sat down in the den, and Dar started talking. "It is hard to be a king, helping everyone with their difficulties. So many people saying 'your grace' and 'your majesty' and sometimes 'my lord.'"

"The snack, my lord," said Melendi, who dropped a dead rabbit on the ground.

Darondo sighed. "Thank you."

Melendi left them, and Dar turned back to Yellow.

"When a king gets old, he needs a replacement. That's where Neomeon history comes in. The first Neomeon king, Dohonda, said this when he was very old: "I am old. I am fading away slowly, waiting for darkness to overcome me. But I must select a replacement, a leader of the great mountain lions. So this is how he or she will be chosen: There will be a test of great courage and willpower, not just for the would-be king, but also for his or her mother. If his or her mother names her cub starting with the letter D, the cub will be given a test when old enough. But it will be dangerous. There is a chance of death."

"Wow!" exclaimed Yellow. "You took that test?"

"Yes, but I am about to tell you a secret that I have not told anyone," Darondo whispered. "The test is something… but nothing."

"Something, but nothing?"

"How do I explain… The test is for the cub's mom only – to see if she will give her cub a name starting with D. And for the cubs… they have to keep a secret."

"But you just told me!"

"You are not a mountain lion. Come with me."

Dar walked out of the den and went into the one next door. In it was a newborn cub.

"She is my daughter, Diamond."

5. BUFFA-DAY

"Come on, Yellie," shouted Diamond.

"Coming, Di," Yellow replied.

Yellow and Diamond had become good friends, and Yellow visited the Neomeon Mountains as much as she could. It had been two years since she had talked with Darondo. She swore never to tell Di the secret of the test. Yellow spent so much time with the mountain lions that she had started to talk like them.

"By Dohonda's name, that's a big buffalo!" exclaimed Yellow.

It was Buffa-Day, a favorite mountain lion holiday when all mountain lions hunt buffalo. Whoever catches the biggest one gets to be the second king or queen for a day, and the buffalo is displayed for all to see. Yellow knew that tonight would be the feast and that all of the mountain lions - and Yellow - would eat the buffalo. Melendi had caught the big buffalo this year. In fact, it was the second largest buffalo ever hunted and killed. The winning hunter also gets to name the biggest buffalo. Melendi had named hers Colo. The mountain lions even began to call it the Year of Colo.

Yellow had become a very good hunter, herself, and she had snagged a good-sized buffalo. But it wasn't big enough. Still, she couldn't wait to eat.

"Who got the biggest buffalo ever, Di?" she asked.

"It was Dohonda, of course, Yellie," Di explained.

Yellow learned that Dohonda was the best hunter ever. Once he killed a buffalo that was twice as big as Melendi's buffalo. Yellow couldn't stop staring at the beast. Last year, the mountain lion Gargettu had gotten the biggest buffalo, but it wasn't nearly as big as this one.

Red suddenly arrived and ran up to Yellow. "Yellow, we have a problem!"

"What is it?"

"Black ran away again."

"For the fifth time?"

"Sixth," frowned Red.

"But we can't ask the Neomeons to find him," said Yellow, "because it's Buffa-Day."

"I'll do it!" said Di. This was rare for her. Di didn't like to leave her fellow mountain lions.

"Well, come on!" shouted Di, already on her way. Yellow and Red followed her.

* * *

Black was talking to Vron, the vampire bat, who now had a mate and two sons. The mate's name was Evleen. The eldest son was Gatheven, and the youngest was Vilton.

"So how is Evleen?" asked Black.

"She's good, yessiree! She's a bit too good! She's so darn good that she's always complainin'. Yessiree, she mostly complains about not getting little missies instead of sons. Yessiree, Evleen wanted to name them Previn and Proove. I was thinking about introducin' you to her. Yessiree..."

"Vron, do you always say Yessiree?" asked Black.

"Yessiree!"

Black rolled his eyes, but he smiled a bit.

* * *

Di smelled Black's scent on a shrub on Shadow Island. Di, Yellow and Red were on the west side of the island. Black was heading east, so they followed the trail.

* * *

"Want to introduce Evleen to me?" asked Black.

"Yessiree! Come back here at... what's that? Mountain lion!" Vron flew away.

"Yes, we found you! Back to Buffa-Day!" said Di.

"Why don't you ever ask Ray's permission before wandering off? Or at least tell him where you're going?" asked Red. "Come on, Black. Let's get back to Ray."

"I'm coming," said Black, rudely.

"Then why aren't you moving?" said Yellow.

"I'm going now!" yelled Black.

"Let's go then," said Red, as she and Black walked away.

"Back to Buffa-Day?" asked Yellow.

"To Buffa-Day!" said Di.

* * *

Darondo felt faint. "Goodbye, lion king! Goodbye forever!" said a voice. Just then, the brave mountain lion felt a horrible pain. King Darando, leader of the Neomeons, whimpered and died.

6. EXPLORERS

Diamond spent months mourning for her father. No one knew how it had happened. All they found were bite marks on his neck. Since Diamond was too young to be queen, Melendi was the temporary queen because she had killed the biggest buffalo. The night after Darondo had died, the Neomeons and Yellow had attended a Death Ceremony, where they buried the king. As more months passed, it was time for Diamond to prove herself, or she couldn't even consider becoming Neomeon queen.

* * *

"What are you going to do, Di?" asked Yellow.

"That's what I'm asking myself."

"I know! You should talk to Ray. He's smart. He'll figure it out."

* * *

"This here is Evleen, Gatheven and Vilton," said Vron, with even more pride in his voice than usual.

"Hello!" said Evleen. "Hi," said Gatheven. Vilton just waved.

"Boys, this here is my friend, Black. If y'all get into trouble, just go to him."

Evleen spoke up. "Now boys, your father and I are going to go, so you can spend time with Black."

"Yessiree! See ya!" said Vron. Then he and Evleen flew away.

* * *

"So what should we do, Ray?" asked Yellow.

"Prove yourself, huh?" said Ray. Di nodded. "I know a way that both of you can prove yourselves," Ray continued. "But you will have to wait a few days." Yellow translated for Di.

"That's okay. I have twenty days," said Di to Yellow, who translated it back to Ray.

"You can return to the mountain lions. Come back in three days," Ray told her. "Yellow, you come with me."

* * *

"So, what do you like to do?" Black asked Gatheven and Vilton.

"We like to explore!" shouted Gatheven.

"Yeah! Explore!" echoed Vilton.

"Call me Gathe," said Gatheven.

"And call me Vil," said Vilton.

"Let's explore at the top of the valley. I've never really seen it," said Black.

* * *

"Push! Push! Push!" Ray urged Yellow.

"Why do I have to do this?" Yellow was holding up a big boulder, then putting it down, then picking it up with her other claw.

"I'll tell you and Di in three days," said Ray. "Now back to training..."

*   *   *

The three days went slowly for Yellow and Di - Yellow because of all the training, and Di because of all the waiting. But they did finally pass.

"In these few days, I've helped to make Yellow stronger," explained Ray.

"Why, though?" asked Di.

"You are going to ride on top of Yellow," said Ray, "all the way around the valley."

"Yes!" shouted Yellow and Di.

"Yes. I have helped make Yellow stronger for two reasons. First, so she is strong enough to carry you. And second, so her wings are strong enough to make the flight. When Yellow lands at the end of the trip, she will be exhausted, and she won't be able to fly for a few days. Meet me at The Crowhead - at the top of the valley."

*   *   *

Meanwhile, Black and the bats were exploring the top of the valley. It had been three days, but Ray had been too busy with Yellow to notice Black's absence. The trio had explored everything except the back of a small hill.

"Let's all fly over it!" shouted Vil.

"Up we go!" said Gathe, as they took off.

"Dragon! I sense dragon!" shouted Vil after a few moments. "Not you, of course, Black."

Gathe and Vil flew away just as Yellow arrived and spotted Black.

"Black! What are you doing here?" she yelled.

"I'm exploring," Black tried to explain.

"Have you told Ray where you've been?"

"Why should I?" Black scoffed. "What power does he have over me?"

Yellow looked at Black curiously. "He created you, didn't he?"

Black just snarled and flew away.

* * *

"Di! Di! Bye!" shouted a mountain lion as Yellow rose from the ground with Di on her back.

"Goodbye, Krengel!" Di replied.

"Who's that?" Yellow wondered.

"A friend," said Di.

Yellow shrugged.

* * *

They were off. The ground below slowly grew farther away. Soon, they saw the green outline of Sun Woods. They were close enough that Di began salivating at the scent of warm prey. After almost an hour, they left the woods behind and came to Fire Lake. The flame-red water marked the beginning of what Red chose as her territory.

"Yellie, I'm not feeling well," said Di.

"It's probably just the cold," Yellow guessed. They were near border of what would soon be White's territory, where the terrain rose quickly in elevation and it grew cold and wintry.

"No, my belly hurts," said Di.

"Then you probably have a bellyache, I guess."

After another half an hour, they came to The Desert. The red sand and sagebrush of the high desert seemed to stretch on and on until they arrived at Swishy Creek and the marshes surrounding it. The marshes emitted a foul smell, like that of a rotten toad.

"I'm still not feeling too well," said Di.

"Maybe it's the smell," said Yellow.

Fortunately, the smell died away and vanished as they crossed the creek. It was more a river than a creek, though, rushing straight out of Fish Heaven Lake - Blue's soon-to-be territory. After crossing the river, Yellow turned south and the Neomeon Mountains became visible. Aexis Peak, Mount Leo and Echo Mountain - all beautlful sights.

"You will return there after our flight," said Yellow.

"I hope so," said Di, trying not to look down. "But I'm still feeling uncomfortable."

Soon they came to another large mountain. They named it Round Mountain because of its rounded top. By then they were in the middle of Black's territory. Not long after, they began to see the vast waters of Fish Heaven Lake. Next to it was the largest marsh that Yellow had ever seen, lining the entire southern side of the lake.

When the marsh ended, The Plains began. They went farther and farther until they reached the territory that Yellow had chosen for herself.

They soon saw the outline of the Great Forest, which occupied a large section of her territory. Next to the forest was Flower Grove, containing flowers of all different hues, sizes and shapes.

"That is where I was standing when I decided this would be my territory. Beautiful, isn't it?"

"It is quite beautiful," said Di, but Yellow could hear some pain in her voice. The dragon was beginning to grow concerned for her friend.

Not far from Flower Grove was Mount Rabbit, one of the largest mountains in the valley. Next to it was Golden Lake. It was about half the size of Fire Lake. "Funny shape," said Di. "From up here, it looks like a lopsided buffalo balancing on its face." Yellow laughed, although she was beginning to grow tired from all her flying.

A few hours later, they returned to Sun Woods.

"We've made a complete circle around the valley!" Yellow cried. "We're almost home!"

Di wasn't saying much by now, but Yellow could hear her moaning quietly.

* * *

After they crossed the woods, they spotted Ray waiting for them. He shouted from below. "You did it, Yellow and Di! You did it!"

"Boy, I'm hungry." Yellow said, as she landed and looked around for something to eat.

"You won't be able to hunt because Ray said you'd be weak," said Di. She seemed weak, too.

"Don't worry," said Ray. "I'll have Red hunt for you."

* * *

Krengel came running into Dream Cavern while Yellow was munching on a snake that Red had caught.

"Yellow! Yellow! Come quick! It's Di!"

Yellow spit the snake from her mouth and jumped up with a worried expression. "What happened to her? What's wrong with Di?"

"Nothing's wrong with her. Di is giving birth… and I'm her mate!"

7. BLOOD FEAST

Red collapsed on the floor of Dream Cavern. She was exhausted after a long day of fighting practice. But she was excited, too. Ray had said that the next day the dragons would start living in their territories. This surprised Red, but she was happy about it. *Finally,* she thought, *time on my own.*

* * *

Black sat down on his usual rock and thought about how much he hated the other dragons, particularly Yellow. They all were six years and 212 days old. Black had kept track by putting a mark on the rock every day. Still, Black was the youngest - by four seconds. He sighed and thought about the man who had created him.

Who was Ray Huffman? Where did he come from? Black decided to investigate.

* * *

Before she started living in her territory, Yellow decided to visit her friend Di. As she flew up to the Neomeon Mountains, she remembered how beautiful they were.

Di's family had grown considerably. She now had three mountain lion offspring (Di told Yellow that mountain lions give birth when they are about two and a half years old. Now it was four years later). Her children were named Foosila, Crasilla and Dewong. Their mother had become Neomeon queen, and the father, Krengel, had become king. When Di and Krengel had reached an age when they were too old to perform their royal duties, their son, Dewong, became the Neomeon king and mated with a mountain lion named Cadali. They had a son named Dugwe-quah. Most mountain lions called him Dugwe. He was one year old, and – because of the faith his parents had in him by giving him his name – he was the future king.

* * *

"It'll be easy. I mean, what can happen? Ray will see two bats," said Black. "He'll have no idea that you're spying on him."

"I don't know. What about the ghost of Mirtlern?" worried Gathe.

"Mirtlern?"

"The old cave bat," explained Vil. "Legend says that if we stray too far from our home, he will rise from the dead and attack us."

"What happened to Mirtlern?" asked Black.

"It was the day of the Blood Feast…"

"Blood Feast?"

"Yes," said Gathe. "On one specific day each year, the bats of this valley go… well… go…"

"Bloodthirsty," finished Vil.

"Every bat?" asked Black. "At the same time?" He started to wonder what that would look like, and it wasn't a happy thought.

"Every last one of us," answered Gathe. "It only lasts one day. But Mirtlern's Blood Feast never ended - until the Grabbing Trees pulled him onto Shadow Island... and he was never seen again."

"Well, I don't think we have to worry about Mirtlern," said Black.

Just then, he saw a shadow creeping above the trees in the distance. Every part of the shadow seemed to be moving in a slightly different way, and it was getting bigger... and bigger... and bigger.

"Guys... what's that?"

Vil and Gathe turned to look at the shadow. Vilton's eyes opened wide. "Black... what day is it?"

"It's the first day of autumn, I think."

Vilton's eyes grew wide. "Black! Fly away! Fast! Today is the day of the Blood Feast!"

* * *

Ray stood on top of a small hill, cleaning his brand new glasses. His old pair was still missing. He wiped the lenses with his shirt, then put the glasses on. He saw a dark shadow in the sky. It seemed to be swirling and changing shape, and it was coming closer and closer.

"What is that?"

* * *

They came fast and silently. They came at dusk. They came from who knows where. But... they... came.

They flooded the skies, their fangs glistening. That's how Blue remembered it. Their wings like daggers, their hearts like stone, they flew. They set out to kill.

* * *

The bats came from the northeast. First, they arrived at Red's territory. She flew as fast as she could toward Dream Cavern. She hoped Ray was there. Then the bats arrived at the territory that was home to White, who almost immediately flew to warn Ray, too. When the bats reached the Neomeon Mountains, Yellow was having a meeting with Di, along with the other mountain lions. The Neomeons fled into the mountain, as Yellow flew to Ray.

Finally, the army of bats found their way to Blue's territory. He didn't warn Ray. He didn't fly away. He stayed. He stayed to fight.

* * *

Red rushed in, followed by White and Yellow.

"Don't say it. I already know," said Ray quickly, as they entered the cavern. "Are you ready to fight?"

"Fight?" shouted the dragons at once.

"Or course, what do you think we should do?" asked Ray.

"What are they?" asked Yellow.

"Bats. Vampire bats, to be specific," Ray explained. "We must warn the other dragons, and we must strategize!"

* * *

Blue couldn't fly. But he was prepared to fight. His claws were sharp. His mind was clear. Just as he was about to face an army of bats all by himself, his brothers and sisters lined up beside him.

"Wait! Where's Black?" asked Yellow. Nobody knew the answer.

"Ray told us something," White said to Blue. "The bats follow their leader, who is usually in the front. If one of us can defeat the leader, the others will flee. Let's go!"

They were off. Yellow did a spin in the air and then a kodge. Red used her flying skills and made many bats chase her. Then White knocked them out, one by one. But the bat leader dived down at Blue.

Blue dodged. Then he tried a pait, but missed. The leader went in for a bite. Blue tried to dodge, but the bat's fangs sank into his shoulder.

"Grrrrr! I... am... a dragon... I... am a dragon... I AM A DRAGON!"

Blue slashed and the bat fell.

8. VERY OLD RAY

Thirteen years passed. Winters, springs, summers and falls. The dragons grew to respect Blue, especially when they saw the scar on his shoulder. They lived in their territories happily, but every year on the first day of autumn, they fought the bats at dusk. The dragons grew older and wiser and bigger and stronger. In one hour, they would officially become adults.

"Kneel down fair drahs and drais of the valley."

The dragons knelt down next to the small redwood tree that they had raced to when they were very small.

"In exactly..." Ray looked at his watch. "... fifty-seven minutes, you will become complete and full adults. The term 'adult' means many things - knowledge, will power and, of course, bravery." As he said bravery, he looked straight into the eyes of Yellow. "But first, before the clock runs out, I would like to teach you one last thing."

One last thing? Did this mean that Ray was leaving them? But instead of saying that, like she would have as a child, Yellow said, "What must we learn, oh Ray of Knowledge?"

"Ray of Knowledge?" Ray chuckled. "You should call me Very Old Ray!"

"Yes, Very Old Ray," Blue joked.

Ray chuckled again. "Thanks for making a point, Blue." Blue bowed low, as the dragons laughed, especially Yellow. Black made a soft grunt. Yellow rolled her eyes at him.

"Okay then, back to the point..." All the dragons looked up at Ray. "Magic... I will teach you magic."

"What is magic?"asked White.

"It is a type of power - a... strong power, a feeling you get inside you. I will tell you more later. For now, stand in a line in front of me."

The first in line was Blue, then Red, White, Black and Yellow. Ray looked at Blue.

"Blue. Bat Defeater, Joke Maker, Fish Eater. Please say '*Blententice*.'"

Blue shrugged. "*Blententice*... I don't understand why I have to..." Suddenly, Blue rose from the ground.

"You are now experiencing the wondrous joy of flight," said Ray.

Blue raised his snout with joy, but said nothing. A blue bubble formed around him, as Ray turned to Red.

"Red. Fast Wing, Desert Dweller, Sheep Stalker. Please say '*Regarstorm*.'"

Red was ready. "*Regarstorm.*" She, too, floated in the air, as a red bubble formed around her.

The same thing happened when White said *Wringcrest*, but it was a white bubble. Black waited for Ray to say good things about him, but instead Ray said, "Black, please say '*Blegarsleed*.'"

Black sighed. "*Blegarsleed*." Black floated up and a black bubble formed around him. But he was not full of joy. He was full of disappointment.

Then came Yellow's turn.

"Yellow. Sofin Trader, Neomeon Friend, Rabbit Hunter and Problem Solver. Please say '*Yeezling*.'"

"*Yeezling*," she said proudly, with tears in her eyes. It felt as if she were floating to the stars.

* * *

Ray was chanting. "*Blentenice… Regarstorm… Wringcrest… Blegarsleed… Yeezling*. Join!"

The bubbles all came together. A huge bubble formed, more than 20 feet across, like a rainbow sphere. Then it separated into five smaller ones again.

"Do you see, my dragons? If you all join forces and remain as allies, that's when the most beautiful magic happens."

* * *

The dragons had new adult scales, hard as diamonds. They were stronger. Also, they had magic.

"Ray, I do not mean to doubt your loyalty, but… are you leaving?" asked Yellow.

"Leaving? You mustn't be, Ray!" worried Red.

"I am afraid so. I cannot stay here forever. You are old and wise enough to live by yourself."

"Where are you going?" asked Blue.

"I am going home."

"But… isn't this your home?" asked White.

"It is yours," said Ray. "But not mine. Don't worry, though. I will come to visit when I can."

Yellow had tears in her eyes. Red appeared stunned. Blue looked like he was going to be sick. White turned his head away. And Black smirked.

"Farewell, fine friends," said the man who had created them. "I will miss you dearly."

With that, Ray T. Huffman, Ray of Knowledge, Very Old Ray, Dr. Ray... simply walked away.

9. LOVE AND MAGIC

The five dragons stood in a large clearing in the middle of the forest.

"What must we do now?" asked Red, hopelessly.

"I say we have a meeting," said Yellow.

"Very well, but where should we have it?" asked Blue.

"Why here, of course," said Yellow.

* * *

"This meeting has officially started - the Meeting of Ray," announced Yellow.

"What shall we do?" asked White. He was quiet, even quieter than usual.

Blue started talking. "Well, we should live in our territories, as Ray told us. Maybe we should..."

Black interrupted. "Do we even trust Ray? What do we know about him? He could be a... a..."

"A nice human who wishes to help us. By Dohonda's name, sit down, Black!" shouted Yellow.

"Oh, Yellow. It's just like you to sound like a mountain lion. You disrespect your own kind!" Black shouted back.

"For your information..."

"Quiet!" White yelled, which surprised everyone.

"Yes, stop this talk of disrespect and mountain lions. I do not like it!" said Red sternly.

"It is not my fault that Yellow has a big mouth - or should I say mountain lion mouth!" said Black.

"I do not think it is right that…"

"Quiet, Blue!" yelled Black. "You're almost as bad."

"Okay, you went too far. Say one thing, and I personally will stomp you into the ground!" hollered Red.

"Same to you, Red!" Black snarled.

"Oh, you did not just do that!" Red yelled.

"You know I did!" Black answered.

"BY FISH BLOOD AND THE VALLEY, SHUT YOUR SNOUT!" yelled Blue, outraged.

Yellow looked at the ground. Red and White nodded. Black released a loud, low grunt that sounded like a tree falling in a rainstorm. Then Blue spoke in a softer voice.

"Back to the point again. We shall live in our territories, as Ray told us. We may want to… well, we could…"

Black grunted again. "Could what, Blue?"

"We could think about it and come back tomorrow," said Blue slowly, narrowing his eyes at Black.

"Very well," said Yellow. "The Second Meeting of Ray will be held at this time tomorrow."

The dragons walked away - all but Blue, who whispered in Yellow's ear. "Do… do you want to take a walk in the Great Forest… and… and talk about the meeting? Unless you don't want to, of course…"

"Of course I do." Yellow's smile showed happiness and embarrassment.

"Um… okay then. Let's go."

* * *

"Ah, the smell of sweet, sweet honey," said Yellow, as she sniffed a big, golden beehive in a fern tree.

"Yes, it smells great. It reminds me of..." Blues voice trailed off.

"Of what?"

"Of... of you."

Yellow's eyes gleamed.

* * *

Blue came to Yellow's territory and sat with her in her cave.

"Want any rabbit?" asked Yellow.

Blue smiled. "I only eat fish."

Yellow smiled, too. "Are you sure? I won't either. I'm full."

"Maybe a little rabbit leg won't hurt," said Blue.

* * *

Blue lay next to Yellow in her cave.

"Goodnight, Blue," said Yellow. "I will be with you in your dreams."

* * *

"Wake up! Wake up! It's almost mid-day! The Meeting of Ray is going to start soon!" shouted Red, as she ran into Yellow's cave.

Yellow's eyes opened. "We have to go! We have to go!"

Blue laughed. "I'm awake! I'm awake! I'll go get us a meal."

Blue scrambled out of the cave. Red turned to Yellow with her eyes piercing through her. She smiled. "Us?"

* * *

They quickly munched on a rattlesnake - or *rattlesler*, as most of them called it - and hurried to the meeting. "Sorry we lost track of time," Yellow said, as she and Blue arrived together.

White turned to Yellow. "We?"

Yellow did her best to keep a blank look on her face, but she knew White saw through it. She practically saw the gears spinning in his head. Red spoke.

"Let us start the meeting." All was silent. "We have found something of great importance."

Black yawned rudely. "You mean *I* found it."

"Yes, yes. Black found it. It may be of use, for it does hold information. But it doesn't make sense." Red showed what was behind her. Sitting on a big clump of grass was an old, rusted box. It was brown and about twelve inches across. In cracked, golden lettering on top it said…

MAGIC

* * *

"What's inside?" asked Yellow.

"I don't know. It is locked," Red explained. She showed Yellow a golden lock on the back of the box.

"Let me try something," said Blue. He stepped up to the box and put his sharpest finger in the keyhole of the lock. Then he pulled with all of his strength. Nothing happened. "Piranha pudding! The lock's impossible!" he exclaimed.

"Calm, Blue. I will try something," said Yellow, and she stepped up to the box. "Yeezling!" she shouted. The box glowed and spun in the air. Suddenly, like a video projection, an image of Ray appeared.

He spoke: "First of all, this is not magic. It is 2055 equipment. Brand new! It is splendid stuff! Okay, back to the box… There is amazing magic in it. Sadly, I cannot perform this magic. But you can. To open the box…."

Black slashed at the projected image, and it vanished. "I don't trust him."

"Black!" yelled Yellow.

Black was fast. He jumped on Yellow and did a kodge. Yellow dodged. "Oh, I'll get you another day!" Black pounded off to his territory.

The fight had begun.

* * *

Days passed. Weeks passed. Months passed. But life went on in the valley. They decided to just live in their territories. Blue lived with Yellow. The other dragons weren't too happy about that.

"What? Are you mad? What are you thinking? Stop this at once!" Those were the comments that Blue and Yellow heard. Their answer was to simply walk away.

Yellow had a feeling for Blue, a deep feeling. She just didn't know what it was yet. Yellow decided to discuss this with Di, who looked as old as she was when she was four, even though she was now an elderly Neomeon. She really was twenty, nearly as old as Yellow. Most mountain lions only live to be about fifteen years old.

The reason for Di being so old, Ray had found out months ago. Since dragons grow to be so old, and since Di was with Yellow so much, she would grow to be much, much older than any mountain lion ever born. Because Di was now too old to serve as queen, Dugwe was king.

Yellow walked into Di's cozy little den, which used to be Darondo's. She saw Di sitting on a buffalo skin rug, eating a sheep. "Yellie! Yellie! Come in! Come in!" Yellow stepped in. "Where are my manners?" Di continued. "Would you like to share my sheep?"

"Sorry, I'm not hungry, and I don't eat sheep," said Yellow. "All that fluff. Yuck!"

"Very well, Yellie. Why have you come?"

"I have a feeling."

"Feeling?"

"A strong feeling."

"Magic?"

"Like magic."

"What is it?"

"Love. I love Blue."

* * *

"You really love me?" asked Blue with a crazy smile on his face.

"I really do."
"If… if you love me, then I guess I love you, too."
"You do?"
"I really do."

* * *

Blue was her mate. It happened fast. They grew into deeper and deeper love. Then craziness struck.

"Blue! Blue!" Yellow shouted. "I'm having a baby!"

Blue almost fainted.

10. EGG-CITING DEVELOPMENTS

"Bain is an expert healer and an even more expert baby-puller. You'll be fine," said Di. "Your child will be fine, too. Don't worry, Yellie."

Yellow didn't seem too worried, but Blue was pacing back and forth.

Di continued, "I'll love the draco almost as much as you will. And..."

"Di!" shouted Yellow. "The baby is coming!"

"Don't worry. I'm here," said Bain, a three-year-old mountain lion, as she stepped into the cave.

"It's coming!" Yellow was shaking.

Bain talked calmly. "Don't worry. Push! Push! Push!"

Yellow was shaking more and more. Blue stood next to her, looking quite pale. Di remained at her side, and Bain focused intently.

But a baby never actually arrived.

* * *

It looked like a rock -- a rock with a beautiful pattern of yellow and blue.

"A rock?" said Blue, terribly disappointed.

"Not a rock. An egg," explained Bain. "Your child will come out of it."

"When?" asked Yellow.

"I'm not sure. I've never baby-pulled a dragon before. Maybe in a month or so."

"A month! I could never wait that long!" shouted Yellow.

"You can, Yellow," said Blue, stepping beside her. "And you will."

* * *

Yellow had made a nest, as Bain had suggested. It was made of twigs and grass and leaves and many other materials. She stared at her handiwork, then she slowly set the egg in the nest. *Such a beautiful egg.*

Blue entered the cave. "Perfect. Now sit on it."

"Sit on it?"

"To keep it warm. That's what Bain told me."

Yellow sighed. "Okay, then."

"Oh," Blue added, "and I brought you a rabbit."

* * *

Blue narrowed his eyes. He sniffed the air. *Sheep*. He broke into a sprint. Blue saw it hiding under a thorn bush that marked the border between Yellow's territory and Black's. Blue jumped for the sheep, but it ran away. Instead, he fell into the thorn bush. He felt hundreds of needles pointing him all at once. He didn't move, though he heard voices. Blue recognized Black's voice.

"We must carry on as planned. We cannot lose."

Another voice spoke up. "What if we..."

"I know what you're thinking, Gathe. It won't work."

"We do it then."
"Yes."

* * *

Yellow was sitting on the nest and staring into space, thinking about the egg beneath her, when Blue stumbled in with a snake in his mouth.

"Yellow, Black's up to something – something bad. I heard him talking to someone named Gathe."

"Do you know what they're doing?"

"Nope."

"Well, I can't check it out because I need to stay on the nest."

"I'll go. You stay here." Blue dropped the snake and ran off.

* * *

Blue tried to find the other dragons, but Red and White were out hunting together. When Blue returned to the cave, the egg was still sitting peacefully in the nest. But Yellow was nowhere to be found.

Suddenly, Yellow popped her head out of tunnel in the corner of the cave. "Guess what, Blue! I just found a tunnel that leads to a room full of mice. We will never go hungry!"

"Mice, huh? Well, you'll never go hungry, at least. Why aren't you sitting on the egg?"

"I wanted to take a break. It's a hard job, all that sitting all day."

Just then, they both heard a sound.

"The egg!" she shouted, rushing out of the tunnel.

The egg had changed. There was a large crack splitting down the middle.

"Here it comes!" said Blue, overflowing with eagerness.

Crack! The egg split, and a dragon popped her little head out. But it wasn't a yellow dragon. And it wasn't a blue dragon.

It was green.

* * *

"Green!" Blue shouted, surprised.

"And a beautiful green at that," said Yellow.

The baby dragon had tiny claws and a cute, little snout. Yellow looked at it closely. "It's a she dragon - a drai." As she said it, the baby dragon began to make a gurgling sound and started to drool.

"What should we name her?" asked Blue.

"Well, if I'm Yellow. And you're Blue. Then…"

"Then we should name her Green," Blue finished.

11: TO PROTECT THE MAGIC

Green grew up before their eyes. She didn't like to eat rabbits, sheep or fish - only mice, snakes, grubs, birds and fruit that she found near the Great Forest.

She loved her parents, of course. And her Aunt Red and Uncle White were big parts of her childhood. But "that mean, old Black," as she called him, was not a part of her life at all. In fact, she grew to hate him.

* * *

It was a late October morning. The dragons had fought the bats weeks before. It was Green's third bat fight. The first time, she had cried and whined and run away. But Green bragged to her mountain lion friends that she had left the battle to bravely fight off a bear. Bears were getting more and more common in the valley.

It turns out that after the battle, Ray had returned to the valley to see the dragons, but Green had missed his visit. She had heard tales - only tales - about Ray. Like when Ray trained a ladybug and killed a demon and ate a poisonous fruit, but survived. The stories had been exaggerated a bit, just a bit.

The second time that she might have seen Ray, she had come down with a case of bat tongue (a dragon disease that makes your tongue black and your throat dry). So she had been too sick to see him. But Ray was coming back again soon, and she was ready.

* * *

Green was spending time with her friend Jelna, a three-month-old Neomeon. In mountain lion years, Jelna was about 2 ½ years old, just a few months younger than Green. She was the daughter of Grend, who was the son of Foosila, who was the daughter of Di. Yellow praised that highly and was glad that the two were friends. So was Di, who still looked rather young, despite being the oldest Neomeon ever. In fact, Di liked them together so much that she told them they should go hunting. Green proudly marched east with Jelna close behind.

* * *

"Greenie, I think I smell rabbit!" shouted Jelna.

"Sorry, I don't eat rabbit, but you can stalk it."

"Okay, then." Jelna narrowed her eyes, sniffed deeply and stepped forward. Jelna pawed around and found a rabbit hole. "There's no rabbit in here, but I think I see something."

Jelna pulled out an old, small brown box. And in golden letters it said…

MAGIC

"It's the box!" Green said with a shaky voice. She had heard its tale told many times. The words of a familiar rhyme started to echo in her head:

A decision was made: The box we must hide.
To protect the magic that is inside.

Red had hidden the box, and Jelna has found it, thought Green.

"We have to open it!" she hollered to Jelna.

"Why?"

Then Green told Jelna the full story of the box, which she had memorized:

A meeting was called, a story told
By Yellow the Brave and Strong and Bold.
The gathering was known as the Meeting of Ray
Because their creator had left that day.
Red beheld a box of old.
They wanted to open it, with its letters of gold.
As they tried, an image appeared,
An image of Ray with a slightly trimmed beard.
As he was to tell them how to open the treasure,
Black slashed at it in his displeasure.
So there, not long after dawn,
The image suddenly was gone.
A decision was made: The box we must hide.
To protect the magic that is inside.

"Jelna, let's try to open it."

"Okay... I guess," said Jelna.

"Let me take a closer look at the box," said Green. "It almost looks stone, but I think it's some sort of petrified wood with brown paper on the sides."

"Wow! You're the smartest dragon I've ever met!"

"Jelna, I'm just about the only dragon you've ever met."

"Well, you're still the smartest."

Green stared down at the box, the she whispered, "I'm going to tear the paper."

She slashed and pulled and ripped the paper. Underneath, scratched into the petrified wood, were markings -- red markings that glowed, a red the color of blood.

* * *

Green brought the box to her part of the cave, the part that was full of mice. Green loved her little section of the cave. It was also full of hiding places. She hid the box in a dark spot in the corner. For now, this was her secret.

There, she studied it. The first marking looked like an "L" in human language, which Yellow had taught her. Ray had taught Yellow. The second marking looked like a "U" in human language. The rest were squiggles, lines and dots. Green sighed.

"Greenie! Greenie! Ray's here!" called Yellow.

Green perked up and ran with all her speed to the entrance to the cave.

* * *

Green thought a human would look more like a dragon. He looked rather like a shaved bear.

"Hello, Green! Hello!" Ray looked at her with a mixture of excitement and amazement.

"Hi." *I can't tell him about the box.* She knew Ray couldn't remember.

When Ray had come to the visit the dragons, Yellow had asked him about the box and he had replied, "My memory is failing me. I'm sorry."

"Green? Green?" asked Ray.

"Oh, sorry," said Green. "I was just thinking."

"I was thinking about something, too. Do you want me to teach you something that I haven't taught the other dragons?"

"Yes! Yes!"

* * *

"You, Green, have the good humor and scales of your father and the dreams and bravery of your mother. That is what you will need for what I am about to teach you."

"What is that?"

"What I do best. Inventing."

* * *

For the next few hours, Ray taught Green all about the elements and how they can be blended together to form materials that were almost magical. Then he told her about a special kind of energy.

"I've discovered that every tree is hooked into the Earth so deeply that the energy has formed underground paths between the trees. They're like tubes in the Earth that you can ride, almost the way a bird can ride wind currents. Would you like to try?"

Green stood there with her mouth open and nodded.

"Okay, stand on the roots of that ferberra tree and close your eyes. In your mind, picture yourself being lowered through the tree and into the Earth. I'm sure you won't be able to do it at first, but…"

Green did as she was told, and almost immediately felt herself moving downward.

"Wait, Green! You're not quite ready to…"

Green snapped out of it, just in time, and Ray looked relieved. "I have to tell you more before you take that adventure."

Just then, an ear-splitting roar rang out.

"What's that?" asked Green.

Ray's eyes grew wide. "Bear! Definitely bear!" he shouted.

"What do we do?" Green had never actually seen a real, live bear.

"Well, in a situation like this, I think we should… run!"

They ran with great speed, but Ray lagged behind.

12: A STRANGER AND A SONG

Red's eyes filled with tears. She had become used to it. Her eyes were wet almost all the time. The thoughts of Yellow and Blue and the love they shared engulfed her mind. Red slumped her shoulders and dragged herself back into the cave. She was sure no one had seen her, as always. But this time, Green was watching.

Only a few hours earlier, Green had saved Ray's life. The bear had gained speed, almost reaching Ray, who was slower than Green. But Green went back, blocked the bear's path and began to scratch and claw at the hairy beast. The bear had retreated back into the forest, and Ray was most grateful.

* * *

Clouds were forming. Rainfall would not be pleasant for the Neomeon clan. On top of it all, a weed that was used for medicine was growing scarce. Daraan sighed. *Times are hard,* he thought. Then he noticed something frightening. In the bushes behind him, in the shadows, were two blazing red eyes, bright as flame.

"Show yourself! You stand in the territory of the Neomeon clan! I, Daraan, son of Zong, leader of the Neomeons, command you, stranger, to behold me!"

The creature approached and spoke in a high, squeaky voice. "Oh my! So sorry to disturb! Where are my manners? I am Nix, son of Glix, at your service."

"What are you?" Daraan asked. The creature had a gray pelt and a striped black-and-gray tail. It looked like the animal was wearing some sort of black mask on its face, only it wasn't.

"Raccoon, sir! Raccoon."

"What are you doing on Neomeon land, Raccoon?"

"Business, sir. Business."

"What kind of business?"

"I'm a Pollyhemus Hirajae - or, in Neomeon tongue, a Jolly Ringer."

" A jolly what?"

"Jolly Ringer, sir. We are a traveling kind who bring happiness to the farthest corners of the valley - for a payment, of course."

Daraan gave him a doubtful look. "What kind of payment?"

"Only what you can spare. Food. Shelter…" And then he added, speaking faster, "And perhaps a big chunk of your kingdom."

Daraan's eyes grew wide. "Never! Be off with you, away from my kingdom, or death will be your payment."

Nix sighed and walked away, murmuring. "Should have just asked for the food and shelter..."

* * *

Nix kept murmuring for miles, but soon he was out of breath. He rested in a small ravine, very near where the valley ended. Nix took a little nap because he was nocturnal and it was mid-morning. He woke at the sound of a fly buzzing around him (Flies tended to be attracted to him. It was not his fault he stunk so badly).

He sat and thought, but did not see the storm approaching. And he did not see the darkness and evil that would come to the valley that very night.

* * *

Black's voice was like the sound of thunder as he gave a simple command, "Leave none surviving."

* * *

Grunn slowly weaved her way through the brambles to see her friend Nix swatting flies and humming a little song:

I've traveled the valley, up and down.
Most creatures think I am a clown.
But I'm more than that.
You shall see.
I'm not like the little buzzing bee.

"Nix!"

At the sound of the snake's voice, Nix almost jumped to the sky. "You startled me!"

"S-s-s-sorry! S-s-so, how did it go?" asked Grunn.

"Well…"

"Wait, don't tell me. You didn't get it again? Why don't you stop trying to be the king of something. Last time, you tried to be the king of ladybugs. I mean, ladybugs? Really? If you can't be a king, get a job like a normal raccoon. I've heard there are dragons in this valley. I don't know exactly what they are, but maybe you can get a job from them."

* * *

Red shuffled toward the Meeting of Ray, which they held every month, when she saw a dark shape in the bushes.

"Who's there?"

Nix popped out of the bushes and bowed. "My name is Nix. Are you a... a dragon?"

Red nodded at the unfamiliar creature. "And what are you?"

"I am a raccoon. I need... a job."

Red looked at the creature. "How can you help me?"

"I can... I can sing. Yes, sing!"

"Sing?"

"Here, let me show you..."

I once saw a rabbit, as plain as can be.
He was beneath the old oak tree.
Yonder was darkness brewing.
Until came robin, who was cooing...

Red was laughing. "I don't know if I could offer you a job, but I could use a song once in a while. I'll give you all the food you could want. Plus more!"

"That's great!" said Nix, and the two of them smiled. But as Nix looked up, his smile vanished.

Red turned around to see an army of thousands of bats turning the sky black.

13: SEEING THE LIGHT

"Climb aboard!" said Red. She scooped Nix up with her tail and flew as fast as she ever had.

Nix turned green, as he hung on for dear life while they flew through the air. Behind him, the bats were approaching closer and closer. When Nix saw them, he turned white. When Red and Nix arrived at the meeting and told the other dragons, everyone began to panic.

"Thousands of bats?" asked Blue. "We've only fought hundreds at a time."

"What can we do?" yelled Green, who was trembling near her mother.

Everyone turned to Yellow because she usually had the answer, but she said, "I do not know."

At that moment, something clicked in Nix's mind, a feeling like no other, a moment in time that would never be forgotten. Then he said, "I know what to do."

All of the dragons turned to him in surprise, as he continued to speak. "As my father, Glix, used to say, 'You'll never have a good rating if you don't have plating. And the beating of the hammer is the best kind of glamour.'"

The dragons had a very puzzled look on their faces, but they would soon know that Nix was about to become the first blacksmith of the valley.

* * *

It seemed like everyone in the valley could hear the constant banging of metal on metal. The sound was louder than a thunderstorm. To Nix, it was the sound of life. To the rest of the world, it was a racket. But when the project was complete, it was magnificent.

Even though it was made out of trash.

Nix knew that raccoons liked to collect things. Why not make it into armor? Several months earlier, Nix had come across a cave not far from where the Meeting of Ray was held. Inside, he had found a raccoon's treasure – a huge pile of metal cans. He didn't know exactly what they were or how to use them…. Until now.

As thousands of bats circled in the sky outside the cave, Nix went to work. When he was done, he had six sets of dragon armor – one for Red, one for Yellow, one for Blue, one for White, and a little one for Green.

Black wasn't there.

* * *

One by one, the dragons flew out of the cave. (Blue just walked out proudly.) When the setting sun reflected off their armor, it blinded the bats. They all retreated at once. They were terrified by the blinding force that flew toward them.

* * *

Gorn the bat had been picked to be Black's servant. He was happy then, but now he was trembling. Black hated to hear terrible news, but he had to tell him.

Black spoke forcefully as he walked into the cave. "Ah, Gorn. I assume the slight problem has been dealt with."

"I am sorry, master, but no. They..."

Black grabbed hold of his neck and squeezed. Gorn was almost unconscious, but he was able to whisper, "They couldn't... fight... the light."

* * *

When the bats flew away, the dragons knew they had won the day. They hadn't even lifted a claw. They also hadn't yet begun the Meeting of Ray. At the meeting, Yellow was the first to speak.

"We all know who is behind this bat attack."

The other dragons nodded. Nothing more needed to be said.

"How could Black do this?" asked White.

Red responded. "I think he felt like he wasn't getting enough respect."

Yellow spoke again. "Black will try to become stronger, so our armor won't always protect us. But, for now, we are safe, thanks to our new friend, Nix. How can we ever repay you?"

Nix grinned and bowed. "Honor is payment enough... but perhaps you could give some food once in a while... or perhaps lots of food all the time."

Yellow rolled her eyes, but began to chuckle.

"Enough talking," said Blue. "Let's celebrate!"

The dragons removed their armor, and the celebration began. Nix entertained them by playing a song on his nose flute. Blue gave it a try, but he sneezed instead. Unfortunately for Nix, he had been holding the flute at the time.

White found this particularly funny. He thought he was going to laugh forever. Meanwhile, Red sat on a rock, watching the white dragon. She had a sad smile on her face.

*   *   *

"Where is Green?" Yellow looked around frantically. Then she saw her daughter - on a branch near the top of an old oak tree. *Green can't fly yet,* she thought.

"Green, you get down here this second! Don't you dare try to fly yet!"

"I'm not going to fly, mom. I was only watching and thinking."

Green had been watching Red, and she knew what had to be done. Red was lonely. She needed a mate, and Green would find her one.

Her plan was already set in her mind. At night, Green would sneak out of the cave shared by Yellow and Blue. She would then go through Red's territory and then through a small marsh, which would take her where she needed to go.

*   *   *

Green's plan was going well before she reached the small marsh. The plants in the marsh made her itch, and the smell was appalling. She climbed higher and higher until frost appeared on the ground. Soon she found herself in the entrance to Red's future mate's cave. She walked in slowly, her eyes getting used to the darkness. Then she saw the dragon she was looking for -- White.

White rarely showed his feelings. It was unusual to find him too happy or sad or mad or glad or even lonely. But when Green saw him laughing at the celebration earlier that day, she could see that White glanced at Red.

White was sleeping, but Green tapped his wing with her snout. White rolled over and kept sleeping. Green rolled her eyes. Then White began to wake up.

"Green is that you? What are you doing in my territory this late at night? Does your mother know you're here?"

"White, I have something to ask you: Red is... lonely and... well... are you... lonely, too?"

White stared at Green, wide-eyed. Then he answered. "Yes. Yes I am."

* * *

The next morning, Green arrived at Red's cave, with White right behind her. As the two adult dragons began to talk, Green slowly stepped backwards and began to sneak away.

Both dragons noticed, but they pretended not to see. They wanted to continue the conversation. As Green walked away, her walk became a strut. She held her head up high. *Red and White are in love.*

14: LIFE AND DEATH

Months passed, and all the dragons were expecting White and Red to have a nice pink baby - or a *draco*. Green couldn't wait to have someone else to play with. There was also no sign of Black's bat army, but they didn't know that Black had another plan in mind.

* * *

Black snarled. *Another draco!* Then an idea hit him. He rushed from his cave, his claws as sharp as ever.

* * *

Ray was visiting again. He walked through the valley (by now, he was using a cane). As he was admiring the scene all around him, Black jumped out.

"Black, why are you here?"

"Why else?" Black answered. In the blink of an eye, he swiped his claw at the man who had created him. Ray fell to the ground, lifeless.

* * *

At that very moment, Red and White finally had their baby. A draco was born, but because such evil had happened that day, it wasn't a pink draco. It was something darker. Purple.

* * *

Green was happy to have a new playmate, but everybody else had been unhappy for months - ever since Dr. Ray T. Huffman had suddenly disappeared. No one could find him. All wondered what could possibly have happened to him. It was the great mystery of Dragon Valley.

Green was now five and already quite mature. She had been working hard to decipher the markings on the magic box. On a late evening in mid-winter, she suddenly realized something. Maybe the shape of the markings didn't matter. Maybe only the color mattered. *The markings are red – not the color of blood, but the color of love,* she realized. Could this help her open the box?

* * *

Purple was a nice enough drai. Not perfect, though. No dragon was perfect. Purple considered herself one step down from not perfect. Her tail was thick and had a shovel-shaped tip. She was also quite chubby. Purple spent some time with Green, but the only creature who really made her feel comfortable was not a dragon at all. It was Nix. He was getting quite old for a raccoon, but he came to see Purple every day and talked to her about blacksmithing.

"The beating of a hammer is the best kind of glamour," he always said. But one day he didn't arrive. Purple waited and waited until finally Nix's friend,

Grunn the snake, showed up instead. "S-s-so very s-s-sorry to tell you this, Purple," he said. "Nix has passed away."

For the rest of the day, Purple wept and wept and wept for what seemed like forever. After she could give no more tears, she made a decision. She would run away.

* * *

That night, she did just that. She ran. She ran southeast across a river and kept going. She saw a figure standing there. In the darkness, she couldn't make out who it was.

The figure spoke. "Hello, little one. My name is Black. Why are you so far away from your mother and father?"

There was one more problem with Purple. She was very shy. "I… I… I…"

"Oh, it doesn't matter. Come into my cave," Black said, as he walked into the darkness.

* * *

Purple stayed with Black. The other dragons looked for her. Red and White spent so much time looking that they barely ate or slept. Part of Purple missed them, but another part of her didn't seem to care. Any time a dragon came near her during a search, Purple hid.

One day, she saw her mother crying next to a river. The sight almost made her want to show herself. But she didn't.

Her true master was Black.

* * *

Green was dreaming. She was dreaming about love, which was the key to the box. *Love is the key.* Green suddenly woke up. Then she saw something that made her heart leap. The box had opened.

* * *

Everything in the valley felt the magic spreading that night - from the largest mountain lions to the smallest insects, from the tallest trees to the shortest blade of grass, from the hairiest buffalo to the softest bunny. They all felt the magic.

All of the mountains, hills, rivers and creeks felt it that night. The magic felt them, too. It spread to the farthest corners of the valley. The valley was the magic, and the magic was the valley.

The valley was truly magical.

PART 2:
THE SECOND AGE

15: FROGLEAP

Thirty years passed. The dragons finally found out what the magic was. It assured a future of many dragon generations. Dragon eggs began to appear throughout the valley, representing all of the dragon colors. There were red dragons and white dragons, blue dragons and yellow dragons, purple dragons and green dragons.

But there was still only one black dragon.

The dragons formed tribes, which began a new age in Dragon Valley. As the new age dawned, there were six dragons in each tribe. They was a Leader (Red, Yellow, White, Blue, Green and Purple), a Prince or Princess (who was in charge when the leader was gone), a Healer (taught by the Neomeon healers), a Hunter (in charge of hunting prey for the tribe), a Sofin Trader (a sort of tribe banker) and a Battle Dragon (you can guess what that is). Although Black didn't have a tribe, he took control of the purple tribe, which lived in his territory.

Although she was still only 35 years old, quite young for a dragon, Green had her own territory now and her own tribe. Evening was the favorite time of day for every green dragon. Everyone was in a fine mood. The sunset over Fish Heaven Lake was beautiful. All was peaceful. But Frogleap, the youngest tribe member, had a favorite part during that favorite time of day - the stories their leader told him.

Green loved Frogleap and treated him like a son. Frogleap was a sofin trader, and Green knew that as the years passed he would grow very wise. Frogleap walked into Green's cave, which was in the side of a hill surrounded by tall trees.

"Frogleap! Right on time. Let's not stay in this dusty old place. Let's take a walk in the Great Forest. I have been planning a great story to tell you..."

* * *

On their way to the forest, they passed the green tribe's healer. She wasn't healing, however. She was sitting on her eggs. They were bound to hatch any day now. Cherryfly had mated with Rohawk, the hunter, a few months earlier.

As Green and Frogleap passed, they saw Rohawk carrying a juicy, plump field mouse by its tail in his teeth. Rohawk was the oldest dragon in the tribe, besides Green. He was bitten by a rattlesler, a particularly fearsome snake, when he was 17. He was never the same. Rohawk could never sleep well, which caused his eyes to turn red. He didn't talk much, other than a slight word here and there. Yet he was a nice enough fellow with a good heart, and Frogleap guessed that's why Cherryfly loved him.

Rohawk ignored them as they passed. He just muttered something and walked on.

"Rohawk's a strange one," said Green, half in thought.

This was something Frogleap least expected a tribe leader to say, so he took the role of tribe leader himself in his instance. "Rohawk is a good drah, just..."

The two dragons said the word at the same time: "Different."

Green smiled. "Let's start the story, shall we?"

* * *

Green asked the same question every time she started to tell a story to Frogleap: "Would you like a story you have heard or haven't heard?"

Frogleap usually picked a story he had heard before and enjoyed. But today he wanted a new one.

"For some reason, I knew you would choose that," said Green. "I'll tell you the story of when the first dragons learned how to fly." She chuckled. "I wasn't even born yet."

So Green told how Red had won the first dragon race and had received a rock as a reward. Yellow had come in second. Her prize was a leaf. And when Green told Frogleap that Black had come in third, receiving a twig, Frogleap snarled.

When the story ended, Frogleap returned to his cave to sleep.

* * *

Frogleap awoke with a start. He had an idea. It had come to him in his sleep. All of his best ideas came to him while he was dozing. He reported to Green as soon as the sun rose. When he arrived at Green's cave, he saw her talking to the tribe's Prince, Gongplain.

Gongplain was a stern dragon. He was like a crow – strong, sneaky and, worst of all, proud. As Gongplain was leaving, Frogleap bowed his head in respect, although he did not want to.

"Frogleap, what brings you here this morning?"

"Hello, Green. I have an idea..."

After Frogleap finished telling Green, the tribe leader grinned and said, "I think you should join me at the Meeting of Ray and tell the other leaders your plan."

It was a sofin trader's dream come true. Frogleap had rarely spoken to other tribe leaders. "Yes, of course!"

"Good. I will see you tonight."

* * *

First Frogleap had to complete his sofin trader duties, which would take him through Black's territory. He frowned. But, like every day, he decided to go. Walking through Black's territory was like slowly walking through semi-hardened mud. It was as if the earth would swallow you up at any moment.

As Frogleap finally crossed the border into White's territory, he let out all the breath he had been holding. Now all he had to do was cross White's territory, and he would be at Sofin Trader Place, a sort of market located on a small patch of land between a marsh, a desert and a lake.

As he arrived, he received a warm welcome from his best friend, Mistyeye, a dragon from the purple tribe and a fellow sofin trader. She had a scar running from her snout to her tail. She was a rebel against Black, who hadn't been too happy about that.

Right now, Frogleap had a job to do. There were three main responsibilities within sofin trading. The first job was to find the moss. Then the moss finders gave it to the moss graders, who graded the moss as either A (the best), B (average), or C. There was one grade better than A – an extremely rare A-plus white sofin.

After the moss was graded, the moss graders gave it to the moss balancers. The balancers provided the right amount of sofin to the Neomeons in return for food, supplies, or assistance. At the end of the day, the traders split all of the food and supplies among each tribe.

Frogleap was a moss grader, and Mistyeye was a moss balancer. Frogleap shared his work station – a long, flat rock – with the other moss grader, Gopherhill from the red tribe. On sunny days, the rock was so warm that Frogleap almost fell asleep. It was a good thing that Gopherhill, who was also the captain of the sofin traders, roared as a signal that it was break time.

After a few minutes, it was time to get back to work. A… C… B… B… A… C… *What was that?* Sticking out of the moss pile was the purest, whitest clump of moss that Frogleap had ever seen. He roared at the top of his lungs, "I found an A-plus moss! I found an A-plus!"

16: AN UNEXPECTED VISITOR

After Frogleap's exciting sofin grading, he made his way to his tribe with some supplies and food. As he arrived, he spotted Streakedegg, the green battle dragon. Streakedegg came over to Frogleap, dropped a plump mouse on the ground in front of him and said, "Rohawk told me to give you this."

"Thank you, Streakedegg."

Streakedegg bowed and walked away. Frogleap gobbled up his mouse and looked for Green. He found her near the border of their territory. She was playing a *xiana,* which was a long horn of sorts that could be placed in the crack of a boulder or atop a tree branch. Green had invented the instrument many years before. It was also used for signaling her arrival to the other dragon leaders.

When Frogleap saw her, he bowed but did not say a word. It was a strict rule that nobody could speak to Green while she was playing the xiana. When she was finished, they went on their way to the Meeting of Ray.

* * *

As Frogleap entered Sun Woods through gates that Purple had forged from pure gold found near her territory, he was astounded. When he saw the banner woven with blades of grass by Grunn the snake, friend of legendary Nix the raccoon, he was flabbergasted. It was quite an honor to be there.

After he passed the banner, all he could hear was the low beating of hard, stone drums. *Bum-thud-dum… bum-thud-dum… bum-thud-dum…* The drumming soon got faster. *Bum-thud-dum… bum-thud-dum.* Frogleap felt a shiver run down his spine. *Bum-thud-dum… bum-thud…* When the drumming stopped, Frogleap's heart almost stopped with it. The meeting would begin any moment.

And then they arose. Yellow with her maple leaf crown. Red with her flowing, flame-colored robe. Blue with his shoulder scar. White with his snowflake amulet. Purple with a sparkling silver ring on one of her claws. Green with her dandelion-chain bracelet. And someone unexpected.

At first, Frogleap just thought it was an insect. And as it turned out, he was right. The little insect flew toward the dragons and landed on the tip of Blue's nose. As he often did. Blue made a joke of it, pretending to talk to the insect.

"Do you mind? We're trying to conduct a meeting here." He turned to face White. "Is there something on my nose?"

Then, to Blue's surprise, the insect answered. "Sorry. Is there something on my feet?"

Everyone gasped. Then White asked, "You're a talking bug?"

"What do you want? A shouting bug? A growling bug? A whispering bug? Make up your mind!"

"Who are you?" asked Blue, looking down at the insect on his nose.

The insect saluted. "I am Prince Argvast Gwamba, son of King Luthain Twi Gwamba the Thirty-first!"

"What we mean," explained Yellow, "is... what are you?"

"I am from a race of royal dragonflies. We have just fought a horrific battle against our enemies, the evil fireflies."

"Why are you here?" asked Frogleap. He was surprised at himself for jumping into the conversation.

Prince Argvast bowed his head. "Now we've come to the sad part... Almost all of our best soldiers have perished in the war against the fireflies. And, well, our glorious kingdom will fall unless we get help immediately."

Then Red asked, "How can you even fight? You have no claws, no teeth..."

Before Red could finish his sentence, Argvast pulled out a tiny, glowing, gold sword and said, "No one insults my fighting ability!"

Seeing the sword, Red hesitated before talking again. "What will you do for us?"

Before Argvast could speak, they heard a horn blow from somewhere far away. "I must go," said Argvast. "I will speak with you about this subject in the coming days." Prince Argvast fluttered toward his distant kingdom.

* * *

"May we continue the meeting?" inquired Green.

"Of course," answered Yellow. "Who would like to begin?"

Before Frogleap could speak, Purple stood up and said, "A bear attacked my tribe, just as I was leaving."

Red stepped next to Purple. "These Bear attacks are getting more frequent. We must find a way to defeat them, or at least scare them off."

"That is why I have created this," said Purple, the best blacksmith in Dragon Valley, and she revealed what was behind her. It was a bronze sphere, seven inches in diameter. "It's a bear repellant. You just open the lid and…" Purple opened the lid and released the worst thing Frogleap had ever smelled.

"What is that?" asked Blue, clawing his nose.

"A mix of rabbit manure, stinkbug shavings and skunk hairs," Purple announced.

"That's… great," said Yellow. "How many have you made?"

"Six. One for each territory. For a price, of course."

The dragons looked at each other curiously. "How much moss will you want from the sofin traders?" asked White.

Frogleap tensed up when he heard his job being mentioned.

"Only one," said Purple, and the dragons breathed a sigh of relief. "One grade A-plus sofin," she continued.

The sighs turned to gasps. Green stepped forward and turned toward Frogleap. "This young dragon graded the A-plus sofin," she said. "You will have to discuss it with him." She flicked her tail at Frogleap and nudged him forward, whispering, "Don't worry."

At Purple's first look at him, she sneered. "You expect me to talk to this draco, this baby? I'd rather leap into the lake."

Blue stepped in. "Hey, it's not so bad…"

Yellow interrupted, "We will vote next meeting. Does anyone have anything else to discuss?"

"I... I do..." answered Frogleap. "I have an idea. Remember long ago, when Green and Purple weren't even born yet, when you first saw Dragon Valley? Remember when Ray first taught you to fly?"

Red smiled.

"... and when he taught you how to hunt?"

Blue licked his lips.

"... and how to fight?"

Yellow grinned.

"I thought perhaps we could have a big contest... a Tournament of Kings."

As Frogleap explained the idea to the dragon leaders, they were very enthusiastic. It was an opportunity to bond with other tribes in a competitive but fun way. It was decided that the first event would be held when the first tiny cone fell from the Great Redwood Tree. It was growing larger now, that same tree that the dragon leaders had raced toward in their very first competition long ago.

So a tradition began that day. Every late autumn, a Tournament of Kings was held for three days. Frogleap was picked as the tournament director and head judge. He was honored for the rest of his life.

17: THE BLACK LIST

Evening was a miserable time for the purple tribe. It was when Black called a meeting known as the Black Council. Black stood high and proud in a large stone amphitheater on Shadow Island. The purple tribe and the bats didn't live only on his island. They also lived in a marshy area across Fish Heaven Lake. Mistyeye much preferred the marsh, where she could be concealed. On the island, she was out in the open. She felt as if the grabbing trees would seize her at any second.

"Move it!" said Hugeflint the prince, Black's personal advisor. Mistyeye obeyed. She didn't want to pick a fight with Hugeflint. Besides, she was the lowest rank in her job - well, other than the tribe healer. At least, that's how Black viewed it. He felt that dragons were too great for healing. He had a favorite saying: "If we need healing, we are weak." Their healer was Min. She was hated by everybody in the tribe. Mistyeye was her only friend.

Mistyeye hated the ranking system that Black had devised, especially when she discovered that the other tribes didn't do it. She wanted to run away to the green tribe and live with Frogleap. *Ah… Frogleap.*

"Hey, Mistycry! Wake up!"

"Crinjay, stuff some grass in your mouth!"

Crinjay was their battle dragon. Mistyeye was only two ranks lower, but Crinjay acted far superior. "I'd rather have a rabbit, but thank you," Crinjay smirked.

"Be quiet, Crinjay," muttered Dangle, the tribe's hunter. Besides Min, Dangle was the only other dragon that Mistyeye cared for in the tribe.

"Thanks, Dangle," she said, quietly. Dangle simply nodded.

Mistyeye entered the amphitheater. It was filled with bats flying all around, a normal sight for Mistyeye. Black stepped forward, followed by Purple.

"Sit!" commanded Black. No one disobeyed.

Black continued. "We have much to discuss. Let us begin with…"

A random bat interrupted. "What about Purple's bear repellant?" He flew near Black's head. Black grabbed him and crushed him in his fist. "Any more questions?"

No one answered.

"Good. Now back to Purple. I admit she has done a fine job lying to the other dragons." Mistyeye gasped. She'd had no idea.

Black showed his teeth as he talked. "The other dragons are mindless as a newborn draco to think that this so-called bear repellant works when actually it attracts the *Grizz* instead. That will give us power over the bears. And we'll also get A-plus sofin in return."

Now I have power over the bats, the Purple tribe and the bears, he thought. He raised his voice. "Now it is time for us to conquer the Neomeons!"

Bats cheered wildly in every direction. Mistyeye had heard enough. Forget about the purple tribe. Forget even about Min and Dangle. She was running away.

* * *

Black was pleased with himself. He would soon have power over the entire valley. How soon was soon? It didn't matter as long as he achieved it. Besides, he had a to-do list of his diabolical plan carved into his cave wall. Black read over it:

1. Destroy Ray. *All taken care of.*
2. Gain power over bats. *No bat would dare to insult him.*
3. Gain trust from Purple and power over her tribe. *Done.*
4. Trick Grizz to be on his side. *The "bear repellant" should take care of that.*
5. Convince the Neomeons to join him. *I shall do it soon.*
6. Make army as strong as possible. *Purple will make weapons and armor for bats, the purple dragons, the Grizz and the Neomeons.*
7. Attack.

* * *

Black snarled. He hated to look at the Neomeon Mountains. He heard a shout from a nearby mountain peak and knew that a Neomeon guard had seen him. Minutes later, he stood in their halls. Dare, the great Darondo's great grandson, glared at him from atop his throne. But Dare was not Darondo. He preferred power and riches over honor and loyalty.

"Why do you set foot in the halls of Neomeons, Black?"

Black grimaced. "I have come to ask a favor. Actually, it's more of a favor to you. Instead of killing you, I have come to ask you to join my undefeatable empire."

Dare was enraged. "Nothing you could give me would make me join your bat-palooza."

"How about an A-plus sofin," said Black.

Dare stood up and stared for a moment. "A-plus?" He grinned. "Then we may have a deal after all."

* * *

Dare may have liked his decision, but many Neomeons did not. In fact, they split into three groups, which wound up creating three separate factions within the kingdom. The Lios Neos (Light Neomeons) refused to join Black in his quest for power. They re-settled in Mount Leo. The Svart Neos (Dark Neomeons), who lived in Echo Mountain, were eager to follow their leader and gain riches. Finally, a small group, the Caivat, opted for neither side. They lived in the smallest mountain, Aexis Peak.

Black had not succeeded in converting all of the Neomeons to his side. But he had succeeded in disbanding a group that had been one peaceful family for scores of generations.

18: RORWAIN'S RUN

It was the middle of the night in the red tribe. There was not a sound other than a hootie's hoot in the distance. Then suddenly, hundreds of roars shook the valley, and dozens of bears (or Grizz, as they called them) charged into the tribe from all sides. A giant battle began.

In a cave, a couple of Grizz cornered Tinwain, the hunter of the tribe. Her nine-year-old drah Rorwain was closer to the cave entrance. Tinwain quickly hollered, "Run, Rorwain! Run! Hurry! I will battle them off!"

Rorwain hesitated.

"Go!"

Rorwain ran from the cave and tried to fly into the night. But in his haste, he misjudged the cave entrance and banged his left wing against the cave wall. Although it was not a small injury, adrenalin took over, but only for a while.

* * *

Rorwain's wing was aching. He could not fly any longer. He landed next to a stream and dipped his head into the flowing waters. He raised his head, just as the sun rose into the sky, and realized he didn't know exactly where he was. But he could barely sniff the scent of some sort of tribe ahead. Moments later, a young dragon emerged from a bush and spoke.

"Hello, I'm Frogleap. What is your name, and what brings you to the tribe of Green?"

"I'm… I'm Rorwain from the red tribe… What were you doing in that bush?"

Frogleap answered, "Mouse hunting. Not easy. The important thing is to find out why you are here… and without a parent."

Rorwain shuddered, but did not speak. Frogleap continued to talk. "Come talk to Green. You can tell her why you are here." He led Rorwain through the trees. Frogleap knew something was wrong, but he tried to not to show it.

As Rorwain entered the territory, a number of green dragons turned to stare at him. After passing through the woods, they came to a tall oddly-shaped hill with a cave in the center. An intelligent-looking green dragon came out of the darkness.

"Frogleap, where have you been?" Green's eyes wandered to Rorwain. "And who is this young red dragon?"

Frogleap quickly responded. "I was hunting mice in the woods when I stumbled upon this young dragon."

"Rorwain! I'm Rorwain!"

"Yes, Rorwain," Frogleap continued. "He would like to tell you why he is here."

Rorwain began by announcing himself, "I'm Rorwain, drah of Flipedge, the battle dragon, and Tinwain, the hunter. I am the first of my generation in the red tribe. Last night, my tribe was attacked by dozens of Grizz, the most I have ever seen."

Green and Frogleap were now staring down at him intently. Rorwain continued to explain. "I was able to escape in time." He looked down. "I do not know what happened to the others."

Green and Frogleap looked at each other for a moment, then Green said, "I shall blow the xiana."

Frogleap nodded. "Rorwain," he said, "come with me."

When they exited the cave, the rest of the green tribe members were already there. They had suspected that something was wrong. For a few moments, Rorwain and Frogleap stood there, overlooking the tribe. Then they heard a loud, low sound that echoed through the valley.

Green walked up and said, "I have blown the xiana. There has been a Grizz attack in the red territory. Streakedegg, you must fly toward our red friends and find out what has happened. For now..." she turned her attention to Rorwain. "This young dragon will stay with us."

* * *

Streakedegg soon returned and told the green tribe, "The red tribe is safe, but Grizz have taken over the land near Dream Cavern and are on the move into the Great Forest."

Rorwain looked at Green. "I don't think I can fly. My wing is injured. I don't think I can make it home without having to land often. And with the Grizz there..."

Green held up a claw to show that she understood and addressed her tribe. "Rorwain will not be able to go back to his tribe the way he came. The only other way to go is to walk... through Black's territory."

* * *

After a few hours, Green devised a route to get back to Rorwain's red tribe. They would begin by heading southeast and then crossing the marsh into Black's territory. Then they would travel along the southeast border into White's territory. Next they would cross the river that leads into Fish Heaven Lake. Finally, Rorwain would arrive into his own territory, joining the red tribe again.

Frogleap and Rohawk were chosen to accompany him. When Rorwain first set eyes on Rohawk he could tell this dragon was different. Rorwain's first hint was Rohawk's eyes. They were as red as the evening sunset. It would be interesting to travel with him.

* * *

As the three travelers neared the marsh on the border of Black's territory, Rohawk motioned for them to stop. "We should stay here for the night. I will scout ahead."

Rorwain eagerly agreed. He was exhausted. After Rohawk left, Frogleap and Rorwain sat at the base of a tree, each nibbling on small field mice that Rohawk had caught along the way. After finishing, Frogleap turned to Rorwain and began to speak.

"What do you think of Rohawk?" he asked. "I saw the look on your face when you first saw him. I bet you thought he was odd."

"It's true," Rorwain replied. "I did think he was different. I trust and respect him, though. Do you?"

"Completely," Frogleap smiled.

They chatted for a while until it grew dark. "Where's that mouse-leapin' drah, anyway?" Frogleap asked. "The sun has already set."

"Should we try to find him?" asked Rorwain.

Frogleap considered for a moment, then stood up tall. "Let's go."

* * *

They wandered through the marsh for some time. Finally, they found Rohawk. He was staring wide-eyed at three shadows behind an overgrown bush. Rorwain heard a quiet cackle through the blustery breeze. Then in a flash, numerous things happened at once. Black and two of his bat soldiers emerged from behind the bush. As they began to rush toward the three dragons, a gray dragon leaped out of nowhere and landed on Frogleap. They rolled into a deep ditch, a falling flash of green and gray that disappeared into the darkness.

Rorwain turned back toward Black and the bats. They were almost upon him. The bat soldiers grinned and bared their fangs. Rorwain began to wonder what it would be like to die. Suddenly, time seemed to slow. Rohawk leaped in front of Rorwain. The bats' fangs sank deep into Rohawk's throat. He fell to the ground, limp.

"Rohawk! Rohawk!" Rorwain cried weakly. The bats used their teeth to imprison the young dragon with metal bands forged by Purple. "Rohawk…" he called once more.

19: ROHAWK'S REQUEST

Frogleap opened his eyes. He was dizzy from the long roll down into the ditch. Everything was a blur. He saw the gray figure of a dragon behind him.

"Who... are you?" He rubbed his eyes with his claws. "I've never heard of a gray dragon before."

"Frogleap, it's me, Mistyeye!"

"Mistyeye!" He nearly hugged his fellow sofin trader from the purple tribe. "It can't be you! You are... you are..."

"Gray. I know."

"But... how?"

"It's a long tale. I'm weary anyway. I've been on the move for days."

"Have you stayed here long?" asked Frogleap.

"Only a night," she replied. "I have built a temporary shelter on the shore of Fish Heaven Lake, farther into the marsh. I was attempting to hunt when I came upon you and your friends being attacked by Black and his minions. I... tried to save you." She smiled shyly.

"Mistyeye, you have my most sincere gratitude," Frogleap smiled back. "But I have to find my friends."

"I will come with you."

The ditch was so narrow that there was no room to spread their wings and fly. So together, Frogleap and Misteye struggled to climb the steep, sandy walls.

Frogleap looked at the starry sky while he climbed. He realized he hadn't slept in quite a while.

As he reached the top of the ditch, he was almost overcome by exhaustion. But his worry for his friends gave him energy. Immediately, he saw the body of Rohawk, sprawled motionless. Frogleap rushed to him.

"Rohawk! Rohawk!"

The great green dragon moved slightly. He opened one eye. It was even redder than usual.

"Frogleap," he whispered. "You must..."His voice drifted off.

"What?" Frogleap asked, leaning close to Rohawk. "I must... what?"

"Watch over my children... when they are born. Keep them safe."

He closed his one red eye and was silent for a moment. Then he opened it for the last time. "And tell Cherryfly... that I will watch her forever... like a star in the sky."

* * *

Frogleap couldn't speak. Mistyeye came over to comfort him. "I am very sorry, Frogleap... Where is your other friend, the red dragon?"

The brave green dragon lifted his head with a jerk. "Rorwain!" he called. There was silence. "RORWAIN!"

They began to search along the border of Black's territory and soon found a long stone wall running along its boundary.

"Black has used a lot of bats to build this wall," Mistyeye explained. She pointed a few hundred feet away. "There's a gate over there. Not that most dragons need a gate, but… "

When they arrived at the black metal door, the gate into Black's territory, they noticed claw marks on the wall on the door. "I have never seen those before," said Mistyeye. "It looks like they have taken Rorwain prisoner."

Frogleap slumped his shoulders. Rorwain was his responsibility. He had failed.

"Come on," said Mistyeye. "There is nothing we can do right now. We're both tired. I'll lead you to my shelter. We'll formulate a plan there."

* * *

Frogleap's first sight of the large lake was marvelous. Small waves crashed as gently as falling snow. For a moment, he thought he was a blue drah.

"It is beautiful isn't it?" said Mistyeye.

"It's amazing," said Frogleap, looking around in awe.

"The shelter is a bit farther down," Mistyeye told Frogleap. "There we can talk."

Frogleap and Mistyeye strode along the beach before reaching the small, wooden hut that was Mistyeye's shelter. Small for a dragon, anyway.

"Come in. It's a little cramped, but it's not so bad."

Inside the shelter, it was warmer than Frogleap expected. There was a small pile of mice in the corner.

"I found the wood in the marsh," Mistyeye explained.

"So Mistyeye. You have many things to tell me," said Frogleap. "What happened?"

* * *

Mistyeye began: "I first decided to leave my tribe about a week ago. It was when Black was having a meeting. I just couldn't stand him any longer. The repellant that Purple gave to all the tribes doesn't make the Grizz go away. It actually attracts them."

"That's why Rorwain's tribe was attacked!" exclaimed Frogleap.

"Exactly. Black even got the A-plus sofin you found. I'm not sure what he's going to do with it, but it's probably something evil. Anyway, after the meeting, I went to my two friends' cave and left them the same note deep inside."

"What did the note say?"

"I think I can remember it. It said, 'Dear friend, I have decided to run away from this tribe. I cannot stand Black and Purple anymore. I am heading toward the green tribe.' At the end, I asked them to destroy the note."

"Good, only they saw it," Frogleap said. "At least I hope so. Please continue."

"After that, I crept past the hunter, Hugeflint, and headed for the marsh. I was planning to come to your tribe and warn you about the repellant."

"But how are you gray?" Frogleap asked, still not understanding.

"After about three days, I came upon a small pond. As I got a closer look, I saw a gray drai staring back at me – my reflection. At first, I thought I was going crazy, but I soon realized it was true. And I think I know why."

"Why?"

"Because I was away from my own tribe for so long that I… lost my color."

Frogleap was amazed. Mistyeye continued, "The next day, I went farther through the marsh and wandered to this beach. Then I found wood and built this shelter. After that, I went hunting and found you and your friends. And now we are here."

Frogleap and Mistyeye looked at each other for a moment, as Frogleap said what he was thinking. "Then that means, if I don't get to my tribe in time… I'll turn gray, too."

"We better get some sleep," said Mistyeye. "We have a long day ahead of us."

* * *

It, indeed, was a long day. They were awakened only a few hours later. Frogleap heard footsteps in the sand. His eyes shot open.

"Mistyeye," he whispered, "I hear something outside."

Mistyeye stood up so fast that Frogleap thought she had already been awake. "Let's take a look."

The two dragons slowly peeked out from the wooden shelter. Immediately, they saw big, muscular Neomeons striding toward the hut.

"Are they dangerous?" asked Mistyeye.

"I think they are safe," said Frogleap. "After all, they're Neomeons."

Frogleap walked out of the shelter, followed by Mistyeye. A Neomeon with an orange-brown color, who seemed to be the leader of the group, stepped forward and began to speak.

"Hello, dragons. My name is Tuddthromius, but people call me Tudd." He pointed to his companions. "This is Mull and Koik." The two Neomeons bowed.

"Never seen a gray dragon before," muttered Mull. "Nobody keeps me up to date..."

Frogleap had to stifle a giggle, but he could tell that Mistyeye was giggling inside, too.

Tudd continued, "We are a group of Neomeons sent from the Caivat..."

"Caivat?" Frogleap interrupted.

"Yes. The Caivat are a group of few dozen Neomeons who have joined to try to stop the war between the Lios Neos and Svart Neos."

"Lios and Svart Neos? What are you talking about," asked Mistyeye.

"So it hasn't reached dragon ears, eh?" said Koik. "Let us sit and answer your questions, shall we?"

* * *

Tudd, Mull and Koik spoke for several minutes, explaining how Black had visited Dare, King of the Neomeons, offering the A-plus sofin if the Neomeons joined him and how Dare had agreed. This caused the Neomeons to split into three groups – Lios Neos (the Neomeons who didn't want to join Black), Svart Neos (who wanted to join Black) and the Caivat (who just wanted peace between the two factions).

When the mountain lions finished the story, Mistyeye asked, "So why are you here?"

"We are here to find dragons who are willing to help us stop the Neomeon War. We have been sent by

Di, our beloved former queen who is now the leader of the Caivat."

"Di is still as young as a newborn bee!" said Mull. "Bright as the sun she is."

There was a moment's pause, and then Frogleap said, "Yours is a noble cause. We must discuss this at the next Meeting of Ray. We will find a way to send a message to you afterward."

Tudd bowed deeply. "Until we meet again," he said, and he and his companions raced into the darkness of the marsh.

20: WANTED

After the Caivat Neomeons departed, Frogleap and Mistyeye started heading toward the green tribe. They arrived just as the stars were beginning to dot the sky and just as Frogleap's color began to fade. Mistyeye was relieved.

"We've made it!"

Mistyeye's voice alerted Streakedegg, who was guarding the tribe from Grizz. He jumped in their path. "Who goes there?"

Streakedegg looked at Frogleap, noticing a bit of gray in his green. "Frogleap? Welcome back!" Then he stared at Mistyeye. "And your friend. Why is she…"

"I'll explain later," said Frogleap.

Streakedegg looked over the dragons' shoulders. "Where's Rohawk? He did go with you, didn't he?"

Frogleap stole a glance at Mistyeye. "Yes, he did… He's… well…"

"Dead," finished Mistyeye, knowing it was too difficult for Frogleap to talk about it.

"Dead? Dead? Rohawk's dead!" moaned Streakedegg. His shouting attracted most of the tribe, who gathered around Frogleap and Mistyeye and whispered amongst themselves. The last dragons to arrive were Green, herself, and Rohawk's mate, Cherryfly.

Frogleap approached Cherryfly and spoke gently. "Cherryfly, I'm so sorry. Rohawk gave his life saving Rorwain…"

Cherryfly opened her mouth, but couldn't speak it. She shook her head as if it were a dream. She wobbled, and Green held her to keep her from falling.

Frogleap looked up a particularly bright star overhead. "He is watching over you. He told me he always will be."

* * *

A few days full of great sadness passed until it was time for another Meeting of Ray. After blowing a loud call on the xiana, Green, with Frogleap and Mistyeye, set off for the meeting. As the dragons arrived, Frogleap could tell Mistyeye was just as amazed as he had been when he arrived at his first great meeting.

Yellow stood up and started, "Welcome once again to the Meeting of Ray. Who would like to begin?"

Green volunteered immediately. "If you don't mind, I have a long story to tell." Green, Frogleap and Mistyeye stepped forward to begin their long tale. As soon as Mistyeye came into Purple's view, the purple dragon slowly retreated into the forest. The other dragons eyed her curiously.

"Where are you going?" asked Red. "Don't you want to hear Green's tale?"

"I really must go," said Purple.

White stepped in. "Purple, you cannot leave the meeting."

"I have to go…" She started to dash into the forest, but just as she began to move a sudden abundance of dragonflies blocked her path. There were thousands of them. Prince Argvast hovered at the forefront. "Not by your lily-livered tail, you won't!" he shouted.

"What… what is this all about?" asked Purple, her face betraying her lies.

"Oh, shut your bat-filled mutton-hole. You're wanted in Patroesamenea, the palace of dragonflies." Prince Argvast yelled into the sky above them.

"What are you saying?" asked Blue. "How could Purple…"

Argvast interrupted. "I will explain in due time, but first I think we should listen to Green's story. Red, Yellow, White and Blue looked at each other, each slightly confused. Yellow nodded, and Green, Frogleap and Mistyeye explained what had happened - from the Grizz attack to the departure of the Caivat. After they had finished, there was a long silence, as each of the dragons tried to process the information. Then Red explained to them that her tribe had been able to drive off the Grizz and that Rorwain's mother, Tinwain, was alright. She also said that Rorwain should be rescued immediately.

"About the Caivat," said Yellow, "of course we will help, but how will we send a message to them? If we wander too close to Black's territory, we will suffer the same fate as Rohawk.

"We can help," said Prince Argvast, "since you helped us catch the Most Wanted Patroesamenea Crook!"Argvast pointed his sword at Purple. "Isn't that right?"

Purple said nothing. Meanwhile, a smaller dragonfly began to tug at Argvast. "C'mon, captain. There's a storm coming. We must deliver the message!"

Argvast rose higher into the air. "Wait, Prince," said White. "Why is Purple wanted at your palace?"

"This will provide your answer," said Argvast, and he dropped a scrap of parchment which Blue caught in his teeth. "Farewell, for now!" he was able to say before he vanished into the mist.

* * *

Blue set the parchment on the ground and read it out loud. In curvy letters on the paper, these words were written:

WANTED: THE DRAGON KNOWN AS PURPLE
FOR RECRUITING FIREFLIES TO BLACK'S ARMY

"Fireflies?" said White. He turned toward Red, who looked at Yellow, who glanced at Blue and Green. They all turned to face Purple.

* * *

"One, two, three, four… one, two, three, four… one, two, three, four…" Captain Kunaash yelled while his firefly soldiers flew in formation. "You there," he said, pointing at a scrawny soldier, "come over here."

Except for being a bit smaller, the soldier looked like his fellow soldiers. He was wearing wooden armor and a tiny, rusty scabbard. As he stumbled forward, his bottom grew pink. Embarrassed, he grinned at the captain.

"Oh, wipe that grin off your face. I have a mission for you."

"A mission, sir?"

"Yes. Black gave me a command to find a soldier and tell him to go down to the cells and… remember that red dragon that we brought in a few days ago?"

"Yes, sir. Hard to forget that one."

"You are to go down and get any information from him. Any at all. You know how. Do you understand, soldier?"

"Clear as the sky on a summer day, captain."

The firefly started to fly toward the cells, but Kunaash called after him. "Oh, and soldier… turn your bottom a different color. You look like a buffoon."

The firefly soldier flew away, his butt turning purple instead.

* * *

Rorwain looked at the ceiling of his dark, cramped cell. He had bags under his eyes. Rorwain couldn't remember the last time he had slept. In fact, he couldn't remember much of anything. He had been tortured in ways to horrendous to describe. Black thought he would get information about all of the dragon tribes. But Rorwain refused to give in.

Still, Rorwain felt liked chewed prey.

* * *

The sky was pure blue, as the red tribe soared over the lake. Red was determined to save Rorwain. After a long while, the tribe glimpsed the shore. They were coming upon Black's territory.

"Stay together!" shouted Red. "We're not splitting up!"

They soon arrived at Shadow Island. The tribe all dived down at once. From the ground, they looked like a fast-moving, red cloud. Soon, a young bat noticed them and called for the guards. A large, black cloud rose from the ground and collided with the red one. But the squadron of bats was no match for the red dragons. The few remaining bats fled, as the red tribe landed on the ground, barely a scratch on any of them.

The dragon scouts had done their work well. Red and her tribe went into the cave, where the cells were located. There were only two creatures guarding Rorwain's cell, and they were only a bat and a firefly. The bat held a key. The firefly held a tiny scabbard.

Red slapped at the firefly, who immediately fell unconscious. And before that bat knew it, he was, too. Red took the key and opened Rorwain's cell.

Rorwain looked up and smiled, slightly confused but alert. He was free.

* * *

Frogleap hugged himself for warmth as a strong breeze made him shiver. His eyes blinked open. He heard a soft squeaking and giggling behind him. He turned his head and saw three newborn green draco grinning back at him.

Cherryfly's eggs had finally hatched, revealing a drah (Treepalm) and two drais (Sterlingflower and Hazelblossom). Cherryfly knew Rohawk would have been overjoyed. He was watching, they all knew.

PART 3:
THE THIRD AGE

21: KNOWER

Ten years passed, and the valley's magic was growing stronger. The magic weaved its way into the snakes in the valley, causing them to become much bigger and much smarter (and occasionally much dumber). The snakes were soon called Slitherers and most of them were not very nice. They established a territory in the northwestern part of the valley, taking a bit of both Yellow's and Green's territory. The Slitherers were like bandits. They stole all sorts of things. In fact, they took just about anything that caught their eye.

The Grizz also evolved, but they grew wings and sharper claws. They were now known as Grizzclaws, and they were neither bad nor good. They tended to stay out of trouble, unlike the Slitherers.

The culture of Dragon Valley evolved, too. A new job was created among the dragons. It was called the Knower. There was one knower in each tribe. A knower kept track of - and made sure everyone remembered - the valley's history. The tribes (even the purple tribe) agreed that it was a good idea.

Another creation was Dragon Apprentice Training. It was a sort of school that taught young dragons different jobs. After a few years, the young dragon would choose his favorite job and become an apprentice to the drah or drai. Eventually, when the young dragons became old enough, they would advance to their mentor's rank.

But also at this time, hiding in the shadows, an evil was rising and about to break free.

* * *

"… and that is how to measure the width of a sofin grade B," said Mistyeye to her small class: Treepalm, Hazelblossom, and Sterlingflower, along with Frogleap's and Mistyeye's three-year-old twin daughters Wingsweep and Puddlejump. They looked exactly alike, except Wingsweep was gray (like Mistyeye) and Puddlejump was green (like Frogleap).

Puddlejump raised her wing. "Um, Mrs… I mean, Misty… I mean, mother… wouldn't you have to calculate the length before the width. It seems to me that the math isn't right."

She was pretty brilliant for a three-year-old. "Well, not in this case, Puddlejump. That's how you calculate for grade C. Very good, though. Will you see me after class?"

Mistyeye was going to ask her if she would be her apprentice as a moss balancer. *She's my daughter,* thought the gray dragon, *but she's certainly right for the job.*

* * *

Treepalm walked along a dusty dirt path. A few days had passed, and Puddlejump had become the first-ever sofin trader apprentice of the green tribe. He tried to block this fact from his mind, but it kept seeping back, like water slowly dripping from a cavern wall.

Everyone in the tribe seemed to be better than he. Hazelblossom was on her way to being a skilled princess. And Sterlingflower and Wingsweep were excellent hunters. What was he?

Treepalm would have to choose an apprentice position within a week. A week! It was almost time for knower class. His friend, Jester Mountebank, the dragonfly, prodded him with his white staff. "You just haven't found it yet, me lad. It'll show itself when it's time," he said, as if he could read the dragon's thoughts. Jester was a green dragonfly captain. He was in charge of the green dragonfly messengers. Each tribe had its own group of dragonflies to use as messengers. They were the same color as the tribe they served and were the means of communicating from tribe to tribe.

The purple tribe used bats.

"I don't think so, Jester," Treepalm began to answer.

"Ahem, I believe you mean Captain Mountebank," Jester interrupted. He preferred to be called by his title.

"Alright, captain," said Treepalm, smiling as he lifted his wing to salute.

They both stared at each for a moment, then began to giggle. Never before had a dragon and a dragonfly been best friends.

* * *

The students slowly made their way to the meadow beneath the pine trees in the Great Forest, where the knower class was about to begin.

Jester waved to Treepalm and flew to his captain duties, as Frogleap appeared from behind the brush. Yes, Frogleap was the knower. He had stopped being a sofin trader years ago. Since Mistyeye was a sofin trader for the green tribe now, he figured knower would be a job that suited him.

He strode over to a rather large pine tree with a square-like trunk. The side of the trunk that faced the class did not have any bark. It was just a yellow-white, smooth surface. Frogleap used charcoal to draw maps and pictures on the trunk. It was a sort of white board for dragons, except they called it the treeboard. Frogleap began immediately, not even waiting for the class to settle down.

"Today, we will be discussing an event that happened not long ago. Of course, as you know, not long ago soon becomes long ago. And long ago soon becomes long, long ago." This he said in every class. If anyone asked why, he would answer, "It's important for a knower to know."

Frogleap then began drawing a simplified map of the south side of Dragon Valley. Next, he drew a small path leading from the left side of the map to the bottom. He pointed a claw at the point where the path began. "This is the center of the green territory. As I said, this happened not long ago - ten years ago, to be exact. I was part of it..."

For quite a while, Frogleap explained about Rorwain and the grizz attack on his tribe and the whole tale of what came afterward, including Rohawk's death. Treepalm was mesmerized as he heard the full story of his father's death. Hazelblossom and Sterlingflower were shaken up, too.

No one was exactly sure who killed Rohawk because no one besides two bats, Black and Rorwain were at the scene. And Rorwain still couldn't remember.

Of course, everybody was certain that it was Black and his bats. Frogleap continued speaking after he told the story: "This whole event happened around the same time as the First War of the Split Kingdom." The class had been studying the wars of the Split Kingdom since spring had begun. It was the war of the Lios Neos, Caivat, and Svart Neos. They were now in the midst of their third war. They called it the War of Conquest. The dragons were trying to stay uninvolved in the war, which they did well enough, though it caused many disputes between them.

"Rorwain has a mate, Sparklight, now, as well as two sons. The eldest son, Rage, has been somewhere on the south side of Red's territory. I don't know how he has kept his red color so long… Well, class, we're all done for today. We're learning about the Tournament of Kings tomorrow. Don't forget to study!

Everyone was already standing and began to leave. As the last of the young dragons departed, Treepalm stayed behind. He had to ask Frogleap more.

* * *

Frogleap turned to Treepalm. "Come inside my cave. It's getting a bit windy out here." Without another word, Frogleap strode in front of Treepalm into a small hole between two roots of a rather high-reaching pine tree. The hole surprisingly opened up into a roomy study. The new sunlight of spring pushed against the darkness of the room.

As his eyes adjusted, Treepalm began to see the outlines of many notes and maps scattered across the dirt floor. He turned around to see a large, flat, wooden table covered by more notes and maps. It also contained many flyers about the Tournament of Kings:

See Gast, the illusionist and fortuneteller!

Can you eat as much as a blue dragon?
Find out at the prey-eating contest organized by Blue!

Dare to wrestle Huskoasion, strongest dragon of them all?
Come on over to the wrestling stage if you dare!

"Treepalm?" The young dragon quickly spun around. He had almost forgotten about Frogleap. "I hope today's class wasn't too disturbing for you - about your father's death and all."

"No problem," Treepalm lied.

"You know, Treepalm. Before your father's death, I promised him something." Treepalm didn't speak, so Frogleap went on. "I promised him that I would watch over his children."

Treepalm was astonished. He hadn't realized that his teacher had been so close to his father. Frogleap held up the flyers he had been studying. "I don't just have these flyers because I am a Tournament of Kings judge, you know. I keep them to preserve history, a knower's most important responsibility."

Treepalm nodded.

"I must admit," Frogleap continued, "I have been watching you, as your father requested. And I do believe… you would make a fine knower apprentice."

* * *

Treepalm wandered through the dense pine forest. The last thing Frogleap had said was, "I'll give you time to think it over. Tell me your decision when you're ready. But decide before the official apprenticeship ceremony seven days from now."

Since the second he had walked out of Frogleap's cave, Treepalm had been trying to decide. Being a knower did appeal to him. On the other hand, he might get teased. Knower wasn't exactly the most sought-after position in the tribe. It was more about brains than skill. He couldn't ask one of his sisters. What if they teased him, too?

Treepalm watched as a butterfly softly glided by his feet. Suddenly, he knew exactly whom to talk to.

* * *

"What you decide is your fate. I have no say in it. It is your decision."

"But Jester, I need your advice!"

"Well, it seems the decision is either know or no."

"Jester!"

"Alright, alright, Treepalm. If I were you... I'd go for it."

* * *

His choice was made. Treepalm confidently strode into Frogleap's tree-root cave. Frogleap saw Treepalm immediately and was the first to speak. "I assume you have made your decision."

"I have. I will be your apprentice."

The older green dragon looked positively delighted. Treepalm later told his friends that he swore Frogleap would have done a jig if he hadn't been in such a tight space.

"Well then, drah, meet me here at sunhigh tomorrow to start your training."

* * *

As Treepalm left, he was happy that Frogleap was excited about training him as his apprentice. He proudly marched toward camp, where it would soon be dinnertime. But he soon got a sense that somebody was watching him.

He looked back and forth, but not behind him. Sadly, that's where his "attacker" happened to strike. Before he knew it, he was pinned to the ground by a slightly older red dragon.

"Are you the one who is drah of Rohawk?" the red dragon hissed.

"Why should I tell you, you jumping on me like that?"

The red dragon slowly climbed off of Treepalm. He stood up. "What's your name, kid?"

"You're a kid yourself! I'm Treepalm. Why did you just pounce on me?"

"Think of it as a greeting," he said. "You won't be getting much more than that. My name is Flame."

Flame stuck out a claw. Treepalm didn't shake it. "What are you doing here?" asked the green dragon.

"Well, if you don't mind being a little kinder, maybe I'd tell you," Flame snapped.

Treepalm glared at this new stranger. *He seems dishonest. And his eyes look strange, almost unblinking.* "What's your story?" Treepalm finally said. "I don't have all day."

"Hmmm. What was that?"

"Fine," Treepalm sighed. "Please tell me why you're here."

"Thank you. Have you heard of a fellow by the name of Gleam, son of Rorwain?"

"You mean Rage?"

"Is that what he's calling himself these days? What a stuck-up drah! His claws are bigger than his brain these days. But, he told me some important information."

"Information? Of what kind?" asked Treepalm. As a soon-to-be apprentice knower, he knew that gathering information was essential.

"You know of Rorwain?"

Treepalm nodded. "Of course. He's…"

Flame interrupted. "He's a murderer."

22: FLAME

"This might come as a shock," said Flame, "but I believe he killed your father."

Treepalm exploded. "He couldn't have! It's... it's not possible."

"Really? What do you know about Rorwain?"

"I... I... I know that he was captured by Black and rescued by the red tribe. I also know that he couldn't remember anything about his capture..."

"Lies," said Flame.

"You don't know everything." Treepalm was growing more and more upset.

"Do you?" asked Flame. "Do you really know anything about Rorwain?"

Treepalm didn't answer for several moments. Then he whispered, "I just can't believe it."

Flame whispered back. "I didn't want to believe it either. But I was convinced. And I've come here to recruit you. We will go kill the killer."

* * *

Kill the killer... Kill the killer... The words lingered in Flame's head. Sometimes he whispered them out loud. Soon, they were stuck in Treepalm's head, too, even though he was not fully convinced about their mission.

In fact, they came to call their quest The Killing of the Killer. They set off the next morning.

* * *

A hummingbird flew by a stunted tree alongside a creek bed in the early morning light when suddenly two dragons - one green, one red - attracted its attention. It quickly zipped off deeper into the Great Forest. The two dragons flew low, touching the muddy floor of the creek bed. Flame was explaining to Treepalm what he was planning to do.

"Right now, we're heading toward the blue tribe..."

"Why is that - ouch!" Treepalm's wing got stuck in the mud, and he fell over. Slowly, he began flying again.

"Because we can't do this mission alone. We would be prey before you know it. And besides, the more dragons we have, the more protection. I'm planning to ask the apprentice hunter of the blue tribe. We need a good hunter if we are to have enough food."

They didn't talk for a while, as they flew side by side over the creek that led to blue territory. After many wing-flapping hours, they saw the outline of Fish Heaven Lake.

"We don't want to alert the tribe," said Flame.

"That shouldn't be too hard," Treepalm replied. "I mean, you surprised me."

"You're right. It wouldn't be too hard - if the territory were mostly made up of land."

* * *

"Can you go over the plan one more time?"

"Very well," said Flame. "The hunter and apprentice hunter of the blue tribe will swim to the surface to catch scaletail." (Although the lake was still known as Fish Heaven, in honor of what Ray had called the creatures, dragons had come to call them *scaletails*.) "I'll then distract the hunter, while you grab the apprentice."

"All right, two questions," said Treepalm. "First of all, how will you distract the hunter?"

Flame took two unusual objects out of small pouch that Treepalm hadn't noticed. The first was light gray. It had a handle and a bowl-like shape on the end. "I found this on the edge of the valley. Ray's species used these for light," he said, as he pressed a button on the back. A stream of yellow light poured from the end. "I call it a firestick."

Treepalm was amazed. "Incredible," he said. "Like magic."

The second object was a chunk of glass carved to look like a scaletail. "Carved by Nix, the blacksmith raccoon, himself," said Flame proudly. "I'll shine the firestick at the glass scaletail and a giant reflection of a scaletail will appear."

Flame demonstrated. He aimed the firestick at the glass scaletail. Instantly, a huge image of a scaletail appeared on a rocky overhang next to the lake.

"It does work," admitted Treepalm.

"Indeed," answered Flame.

"How am I supposed to grab the apprentice? What if he yells or starts to fight?" Treepalm asked with a tinge of anxiety in his voice.

"Oh, don't worry about any of that," said Flame, as he reached back into his pouch. He removed a ball that was barely an inch in diameter. It had a silvery metallic color and tiny blue points all over its surface.

"It's called a *chill orb*, created by a group of white dragons. Just throw this at the apprentice, and he'll do whatever you like. Remarkable, isn't it?"

"Isn't that a bit… cruel?" Treepalm asked.

"It won't hurt," said Flame, handing the chill orb to his green companion. "And it's for the greater good."

"I suppose you're right," said Treepalm, but he was not sure how much he supposed that.

Just then, the water in the lake began to ripple. "Get ready!" said Flame, as he jumped behind a boulder. Treepalm ran behind a thick tree in the opposite direction. Soon, two heads broke the surface of the water not far from the shore. Treepalm saw the glint of their blue wings treading water, similar to the frequent flapping of a hummingbird's wing.

Blue dragons can fly, Treepalm thought, *except they do it in the water.* He couldn't think about it much more, however, because he soon saw a giant image of a scaletail appear a couple hundred feet from where the blue dragons were treading water. He heard the hunter say, "Rift, stay here! I'm going to check this out."

Rift nodded, curiously looking at the yellow scaletail image, as the blue hunter dove beneath the surface and toward the image. As soon as the hunter disappeared, Treepalm made his way along the shore toward Rift, chill orb at the ready. He crouched a few dozen feet away behind a collection of large cattails. Then he lightly tossed the chill orb at the blue dragon. It hit his right arm without him even knowing it and then melted into a silvery circle onto his skin.

For a few seconds, nothing happened. Treepalm held his breath. Slowly, six spikes poked out of the silvery circle. The air around Rift grew cold. Icicles grew on the tips of Rift's wings, spreading up to his head.

"What's happening..." Rift croaked, as his head froze. His pupils disappeared from his eyes, leaving pure whiteness. *It looks uncomfortable*, thought Treepalm, who was growing quite uncomfortable, himself.

* * *

What was that feeling? It's my eyes. My eyes are stinging. Rift tried to close his eyelids. They didn't budge. *What is this?*

Attempting to ignore his watering eyes, he looked straight ahead. At first, he thought he was looking through glass. He soon realized it wasn't glass at all, but ice. Rift then noticed something odd. He felt as if he was moving, although he didn't feel his body move at all. He looked back at the ice around him and something caught his attention. There were tiny particles in the ice. They were all moving. Moving him. Moving his body. Controlling him.

Rift saw blobs of color through the moving ice. Two blobs - one red, one green. He soon made out the forms of two young dragons, about his age. It seemed that they were controlling him, moving him farther and farther away from the blue territory. After several miles, he heard the red dragon mutter a simple word: "Release."

The ice melted and vanished in a wisp of steam. Rift blinked. His eyes stopped watering. The green dragon took a step toward him.

"Sorry about that."

23: THREE NEW COMPANIONS

"No problem," Rift sneered sarcastically. "You scale-turning bat-gut. Who are you? Hunter Mormus will find you and report you to Blue. He'll know what to do with you frog-eyed smoke-breathers!"

"Calm down, Rift," Flame calmly said to him.

"Only friends call me Rift," said the blue dragon. "I am Rifttaker, son of Riverpace and Lilypath, blue hunter apprentice! Tell me who you are!"

"Treepalm, son of Rohawk and Cherryfly, green knower apprentice."

"Name's Flame, son of Rorwain and Sparklight, red prince apprentice."

Treepalm gasped. "Rorwain is your father?"

"Who is Rorwain?" asked Rift.

Flame ignored Rift and turned to Treepalm. "Yep."

"So our quest is to kill your father."

"You're going to kill someone?"

"Pretty much," said Flame, answering both of them. He turned to Rift. "And you're going to help us."

"And why would I do that?"

"To become a hero of Dragon Valley," Flame replied. "To become a legend."

Rift was quiet for several moments. He clearly liked the sound of that. Treepalm was quiet, too, but mostly because he was frustrated and confused.

"So Rage – I mean, Gleam – is your brother?"

"Who?" asked Rift.

"Uh-huh. Gleam was visiting me when he told me about Rorwain killing Rohawk. I no longer think of Rorwain as my father."

"Who's Rohawk?" asked Rift.

"My father," said Treepalm.

Rift looked at the green dragon and then at the red one. "Your father killed his father?"

Flame nodded.

"And you're a prince apprentice?" Treepalm asked Flame.

Flame nodded again. "Have been for half a year."

"Why didn't you tell me all of this from the beginning?"

Flame shrugged. "It never came up."

Treepalm slouched down, aggravated.

"I suppose we should rest for the night," Flame finally said.

"Fine," answered Rifttaker. "But tomorrow morning I'm heading straight back to my tribe."

Flame was disappointed. "If you must."

* * *

A crow cawed overhead as ghastly arms bearing diamond-shaped scars grasped at the throats of two dragons.

"Are you not doing what I ask?" said a sinister voice.

"We would never disobey," the drah calmly said.

"Of course not," answered the drai.

The ghastly dragon was surprised that the two dragons weren't shaking in fear. He was not used to this reaction. "Then go!" he quickly demanded.

* * *

"Wake you, you snoring hooties," said an unfamiliar voice.

Treepalm groaned, slowly waking, and saw a mountain lion staring at him. "Who are you?"

"She's Merellia, Neomeon of the Caivat, apprentice healer," answered Flame, stepping from behind her. "We've known each other for quite a while. She wishes to join our quest. Merellia has never been outside Neomeon territory, but I've told her a lot."

Merellia had intelligent green eyes. Her pelt had a light tan color and an even lighter underbelly. She seemed very observant and clever. Merellia stared at the three dragons. She wasn't at all afraid. Suddenly, she broke her concentration and lifted the roof of her mouth to the air, the way Neomeons smell. Her sharp, green eyes grew wide.

"We're being watched."

* * *

Rift was panicking. "Who is it? Is it big? Is it Black?"

"Seems small," Merellia told them. "And it has wings. Maybe one of Black's bats."

"What are we to do?" asked Treepalm.

"We can't let the winged beast get away with any information," said Flame.

"Then we must kill it," said Merellia. She licked her paws. "Wouldn't mind some bat blood."

* * *

"Treepalm, Rift, go into that tunnel under that mossy wood. That's where the bat is hiding," said Merellia. "On my way here, I saw the exit to the tunnel. It's about two hundred feet away. There is enough room for you to squeeze in and chase it out to the other side."

"Where we'll be waiting," said Flame.

Treepalm was surprised that Merellia had taken charge. He was used to Flame thinking of plans, although he agreed with Merellia's idea immediately. When they got close enough to the tunnel entrance, Treepalm's eyes were drawn to the mossy wood covering it. The first thing he noticed was that it didn't look like moss at all. It was completely smooth and had bumps all over it. The other strange thing he noticed was that there was no wood at all, just the smooth moss covering the tunnel. *Odd,* he thought, *very odd.* He couldn't study the moss any longer, though. He was a foot away from the tunnel.

"Are you ready, Rift?" he asked.

"You know I'm going back to my tribe after this, right?"

"If you insist," said Treepalm.

Rift narrowed his eyes. "Let's do this."

The tunnel was damp and a tight squeeze. The two young drahs crawled their way through the twisting hallway. The only source of light was the very distant exit. Treepalm could now smell the animal that Merellia had sniffed out. It was around the next bend.

Treepalm whispered to Rift. "On the count of three, we'll charge the bat and drive it out. One... two... three!"

They both roared and charged around the bend. And they came face to face with someone who was definitely not a bat.

"Jester?" asked Treepalm with disbelief. "What are you doing here?"

The little green creature smiled. "Waiting," he said.

"For whom?"

"Well, for you, of course!"

"I know who you are," said Rift. "You're Jester Mountebank, captain of the whole green dragonfly squad!"

Jester looked impressed, but he said nothing.

"Why are you waiting for me, exactly?" asked Treepalm.

"I've been following you. I saw you meet Flame, and I've watched your quest so far," said the captain.

"Why didn't you reveal yourself?"

"I was just about to, actually, before that Neomeon - what's her name? Merellia? - showed up. She would have cut me into pieces and put me on a stick before she realized I was no threat!"

Neomeons and dragonflies didn't get along. They each thought their species was more superior.

"We should leave this place," said Rift, looking around at the tunnel walls. "Flame and Merellia are waiting."

"Very well," Jester replied. "But I'll be in the back, just in case that Neomeon pounces."

* * *

It was two days later. The three dragons, the Neomeon and the dragonfly were miles from Fish Heaven Lake. They had set up a small camp in the fields of Yellow's territory. The area was very open for miles around, which gave everyone a slightly uncomfortable feeling. They had built a small fire. Flame had told them they would meet a yellow drah and a white drah the next day. Rifttaker kept saying he would return to his tribe the next morning. He never did.

Flame stood up, looking at the flames of the fire. "I just remembered an old red dragon trick."

"What is it?" asked Rift.

"We call it *realflazing*. Here. Watch this." He stared harder at the fire until his eyes turned orange. He then took a breath in, and the flames from the fire whipped around him, like a red shooting star. Flame opened his mouth, and the flames flew inside. His eyes glowed brighter, and he exhaled, blowing fire at the ground. Suddenly, in that very spot there appeared an orange sphere filled with gray smoke. It seemed to be made of hardened flame. Flame's eyes were still glowing orange. He picked up the ball of flame and threw it at the ground. When it hit, it kept going, cutting a very deep hole in the ground. "That flame ball can destroy anything but another flame ball."

"What is it used for?" Merellia asked. She saw that the normal brown color was returning to Flame's eyes.

"We may need a weapon someday," Flame told the group.

"For what?" asked Treepalm.

Suddenly, everyone understood. *Black*, they all thought.

24: THE TOURNAMENT OF KINGS

The others were asleep, besides Rift and Jester. "What do you know about Slitherers?" asked Rift.

"Giant beasts," Jester spat. "Bandits. Rogues. Outcasts. Assassins. Spies. They could be watching us right now. I encountered one once. Big fella. I didn't stick around. I flew for my life." The captain smirked. "I don't think the beast even saw me."

Rift looked nervous. Jester seemed to be enjoying it. He continued his story. "There is something odd about Slitherers that no one has ever figured out. It's like they can pop out of thin air anywhere. Why I heard they raided the white tribe a few weeks ago."

"On the other side of the valley?" asked Rift. "How could they get there without being seen?"

Jester gave a tiny shrug. "Well, no one knows..."

* * *

The sun was only peeking above the horizon when they met the two dragons near the yellow tribe's camp. They were not at all alike. The yellow dragon's name was Beesting, drah of Sun and Honey. He was a yellow sofin trader apprentice. Sting, as he liked to be called, was energetic and friendly. The white dragon's name was Whitelizard. He was quite old, magically born by

White. He was knower of the white tribe. This was an important dragon who had a sense of adventure.

The only place they needed to go before embarking on the Killing of the Killer was the Tournament of Kings, where their one remaining companion was supposed to be. Every Tournament of Kings took place all over the upper part of Dragon Valley. It officially began after the dragon leaders gave a speech together about the valley. The speech always took place at the location of the Meeting of Ray. Every dragon in the valley (with the exception of Black) stood in a giant crowd, eager to hear what the leaders had to say.

The adventurers stood in the back, searching the crowd for their final companion, a purple dragon. Before they could find her, the speech began. Blue started.

"A scaletail swims swiftly and unpredictably, as does this valley...

"Life prospers and gives its magic," said Green.

White then spoke. "Our numbers are rising. In some tribes, there are as many as twenty dragons. There is now a total number of 111 dragons in the valley, and more are on the way."

Purple was next to speak. After being accused by the dragonflies of recruiting fireflies for Black's army, Purple had been questioned for many days by the head of the DJC (Dragonfly Judging Council). Her punishment was to spend a few nights in the dragonfly palace dungeon. Her fellow dragons thought it was a proper punishment. They were very disappointed in her, but they allowed her to participate in the Tournament of Kings.

"New magic and weaponry are slowly being discovered," she said.

Red then said, "We have been here many years, and we still can't resist the beauty of the valley."

"We will always honor the great Ray for giving us the gift of life," Yellow concluded proudly.

"Let the Tournament of Kings begin!" they all announced, and it began.

* * *

Sun Woods erupted into chaos. The good kind. Dragonflies sang and danced, as they flew through the air. Jester joined them. He sang louder than anyone:

Tra-diddly-la, La-la-triddly-dah
Listen closely, every drai and every drah
The Tournament of Kings is finally here.
The competition is getting near.
Humplety, dumplety, dimplety, doo
Yellow, red, green, purple, white and blue.
What will occur? Who will succeed?
We will find out. Oh, yes indeed!

Jester grinned at his new friends. "Before I was a captain, I was a bard at the Royal Palace of Dragonflies."

At that moment, games and trading posts were opening. The Tournament of Kings wasn't just a competition. It was a massive market and carnival. "I have a friend in the purple tribe," said Whitelizard. "He should have a store here, and he can help us find the purple drai we're looking for. He usually sets his shop up toward the west side of Sun Woods."

They followed a narrow, dirt path, passing many things. Blue and a group of blue dragons were having a prey-eating contest. There were fish bones scattered everywhere. The group also passed a jewelry store, a teeth sharpener and one of the tournaments.

The Tournament of Kings was complicated, but Treepalm had slowly learned how it worked from one of the older members of the green tribe. There were several competitions, and the victors were chosen by judges called the Shazar. There was one Shazar for each tournament, and that judge specialized in each event. But there was also a Head Shazar, who served as a judge for every tournament. Frogleap was the Head Shazar.

Ten dragons participated in the Tournament of Kings - different ones every year, each competing in all of the events. After each event, the Shazar picked the five worst competitors, and the Head Shazar chose the five best. The dragon who did the worst received one point. The top dragon earned ten points. The dragon with the most points at the end of the tournaments was named Dragon King for the year and was rewarded with an enormous pile of prey.

The first event that Treepalm and his friends witnessed was the Battle Tournament. There were two large pedestals, one for the Battle Shazar and one for the Head Shazar.

Frogleap! Thought Treepalm. He hadn't seen his mentor for quite a while.

"That's Stump," said Beesting, pointing at the Battle Shazar, a scrawny yellow drah. "He's my cousin. Kind of an awkward little fellow."

Dragons of various colors watched the event, even a few young dracos alongside their parents. The battle tournament was one of the most challenging events. There was a large board that listed the names of the ten participating dragons - Honeytree, Frostbeetle,

Stormglaze, Mormus, Streakedegg, Hugeflint, Firestopper, Snoweye, Spalgrin… and Rage.

"Frostbeetle is my son," bragged Whitelizard.

"I didn't know my mentor Mormus was competing!" Rift exclaimed.

It took Treepalm a second to realize that they hadn't noticed Rage's name. "I see your brother's competing," he whispered in Flame's ear.

"I'm sorry for not telling you," said Flame.

"Sure you are!" spat Treepalm. He was starting to wonder why Flame was reluctant to reveal more information. Treepalm turned his attention back to the tournament.

Four dragons were charging a large, red dragon, who he guessed was Rage. Very large, even for a dragon, Rage had long, sharp claws as black as night and an evil, twisted face. He also had ghastly arms with diamond-shaped scars all over them.

A split-second before the four dragons reached him, he flew into the air. The dragons who had been charging him crashed into each other. Before they could move, the battle ended, as Rage landed roughly on top of them.

Treepalm, Flame, Rift, Beesting, Whitelizard, Merellia and Jester watched the remaining events in the Battle Tournament. Finally, it was time for Stump to select the bottom five dragons. He cleared his throat. "Er, um, Spalgrin receives one point. Good try, Spalgrin." He cleared his throat again. "Er, two points for Snoweye. Three points for Firestopper. Uh, Stormglaze receives four points. And, let's see, Hugeflint receives five."

Then Frogleap loudly spoke. "Thank you, Stump. I have decided that Honeytree will receive six points. Mormus has earned seven points. Eight points for

Frostbeetle. Streakedegg receives nine. And Rage wins. Ten points!"

The crowd of dragons erupted into a cheer. Rage smirked and bared his teeth. Treepalm squinted. *Did he just make a muscle?*

* * *

"Come. We cannot dawdle any longer. My friend's store is very close now," said Whitelizard. It was. Around the next bend, they came upon a rather large, old shack. A tattered banner read: DANGLE'S DRAGON VALLEY ANTIQUES.

"Dangle is the hunter of the purple tribe," Whitelizard explained. "He competed in the Tournament of Kings last year and came in third. He is also very interested in old items."

They entered. It was dim inside. Dust coated everything. As they walked in, a little bell rang. A door in the back creaked open, and a purple drah stepped out.

"Customers? Well, hello Whitelizard! I haven't seen you for a while. Have you come with your friends to pick up some antiques? I have a great collection of pure white pine cones..."

"No time for that today, Dangle. We are searching for a purple drai," Whitelizard told him.

"What is her name?" Dangle asked.

Whitelizard looked at Flame. "What *is* her name, Flame? You never told us."

"Her name," replied Flame, "is Fernpass."

"Fernpass? She just left!" said Dangle. "I think she said she was going to some sort of illusionist a bit north of here."

"Thank you very much for your help," said Flame. "We ought to get..."

"Wait! Before you leave, why don't you take a look around the shop. A friend of Whitelizard is a friend of mine. I can offer you some excellent deals."

Treepalm stepped forward. "I suppose we could have a quick look."

So they did. Treepalm passed Neomeon fur rugs, scaletail scale necklaces, even Slitherer skin pouches. But nothing too interesting. Then something drew his attention. Attached to a wall in the back was something that looked like a maze drawn on a large strip of parchment. Oddly, though, it had about a dozen exits.

"What is this?" Treepalm asked Dangle.

"Ah, that. That's a map of the Slitherer tunnels."

"Tunnels?"

"The Slitherers don't spend much time above ground. They have tunnels that stretch across the valley. Rumor has it that they have an ancient artifact from Ray himself. Sadly, the map doesn't offer any information about where it is."

"We'll take it!" Flame interrupted. He drew out his pouch and removed a small piece of Grade B sofin.

Dangle nodded. "Pleasure doing business with you."

Flame grabbed the map from the wall, rolled it up and gave it to Treepalm. "This could be useful," he said.

* * *

Not long after they bid farewell to Dangle, they headed north, deeper into Sun Woods. As they did, they passed the Flying Tournament. A race was about to begin.

Mormus, the blue dragon, couldn't fly, of course. So he was temporarily replaced by a large yellow dragon. A nearby billboard revealed that this dragon's name was Sevrem. The race began, and Rage quickly sped into the lead, followed by Snoweye, Hugeflint and Sevrem. All ten dragons quickly flew out of sight.

For several minutes, there was quiet. Then, out of nowhere, three dragons appeared. They were neck and neck - red, yellow and purple blurs that Treepalm could make out as Rage, Sevrem and Hugeflint, who was starting to tire and slowly faded behind the other two. It was down to Rage and Sevrem. First, Rage was ahead, then Sevrem found a burst of speed. They were alongside each other again. As they neared the finish, Sevrem drew his wings in and sliced through the air.

An announcer shouted the results. "The winner, by a nose, is Sevrem!" The crowd cheered. Rage landed with a thud near Flame, who nodded appreciatively at his sibling. Rage just grunted and flew off.

Flame, Treepalm and the rest continued on. They soon reached where Dangle had told them to go. It was a part of the woods that contained one lonely stand and one lonely stage. Treepalm walked closer to the stage, inspecting it. Painted in dull red, it said:

HUSKOASION, STRONGEST DRAGON OF THEM ALL!

The name rang a bell, but Treepalm couldn't remember why. He soon realized that he smelled something odd. That wasn't red paint... *Blood! This is written in blood!* He had a bad feeling about this place.

He moved on to the shop, where Dangle said Fernpass would be. Painted in purple, the sign said:

GAST, ILLUSIONIST AND FORTUNETELLER!

This time, it was just paint. *Wait a second. Huskoasion? Gast?* Treepalm had seen those names on flyers in Frogleap's cave.

"Well, um, who-who…" Rift stuttered, "… wants to go first?"

Flame stepped forward, followed by Whitelizard, Merellia, Jester, Beesting and Treepalm. Rift grudgingly brought up the rear. They walked into a hallway made of uneven stone. Mounds of rock and fur were scattered across the ground. The hallway turned left and opened into a small room containing jars filled with rabbit bones and scaletail eyeballs.

"Fernpass? Fernpass?" Flame whispered.

There was silence. No one answered.

"Hey, look over here!" said Beesting, pointing to a rusty, metal hatch attached to the floor in the back of the room. The rust nearly made it blend into the floor.

"Should we take a look?" asked Treepalm.

Flame and Merellia were already clawing at the metal. "It seems to be locked from the inside," gasped Merellia, as she pulled at it with all her strength.

"Stand back," said Whitelizard. "I have an idea."

Whitelizard had always worn a necklace similar to White's snowflake amulet. As he took it off, Treepalm realized what it was – a chill orb. Whitelizard dropped it on the rusted hatch. For a moment, nothing happened. Then quite suddenly, six white spikes poked out of the chill orb. The air in the room grew cold. Ice appeared all over the hatch. Whitelizard stomped his foot on it, and it fell to the ground below in icy shards.

* * *

The group slowly climbed down the narrow shaft, careful to avoid the shards of ice below them. When they exited the shaft, they came into an immense triangular room. The floor was made of cracked tiles, as were the walls and the ceiling. After a quick analysis, Treepalm noticed that a symbol was carefully carved into each tile. One symbol seemed to appear most frequently. It was a pyramid with a many-pointed star inside it. The star must have had dozens of little points.

"Have they thrown you guys in, too?" asked a voice from a dark corner of the room.

The group was startled, to say the least.

"Who's there?" asked Flame.

A purple drai emerged from out of the darkness. "I am Fernpass, daughter of Hugeflint and Min, purple battle dragon apprentice - and a rotten one, too."

"Why do you think that?" asked Treepalm.

"If I was good at fighting, I wouldn't be stuck in here right now."

Two dragons, a drah and drai, stepped into the room. One was red and incredibly muscular. The other was purple with raven black eyes. The purple drai held up an ice shard and shook her head. "Naughty, naughty, naughty. Now what could we possibly do with these?"

The drai laughed wickedly. A symbol, similar to the symbols on the tiles, appeared on the ice shards, glowed bright green and hurtled toward Treepalm and his fellow adventurers. They all ducked just in time, as the ice shards stuck into the wall behind them with a loud *thwack.*

"What is this magic?" shouted Whitelizard.

"Our master R—"started the red dragon.

"Don't tell them anything!" interrupted the purple drai.

Rorwain, Treepalm thought. *He was going to say Rorwain.*

The red drah re-started. "Our master sent us to capture you. You walked right into our trap."

"And who are you?" asked Flame.

"I am Huskoasion, strongest dragon of them all! She is Gast."

"The illusionist?" asked Merellia.

"More like a poison runekeeper," said Gast.

"A what?" asked Rift.

Gast cackled. "You will find out when you see where we're taking you," she said, as she raised her bony claws.

Treepalm saw a flash of green. Then everything went black.

25: SUNDROP'S RIDDLE

When Treepalm awoke, he was lying on a tattered, brown rug in a cell. To his left were iron bars. To his right was a wall made of stone bricks. In the back of the room, he saw a small slit in the wall through which he could see the dim outline of Rift lying on a rug.

"Psst! Rift!" he whispered.

Rift's eyes blinked open. "Where are we?"

Before Treepalm could answer, a voice from behind the iron bars answered for him. "Heh-heh. You're in Grub's Grub. I'm Grub. Here's your grub."

Treepalm turned to see a gray, fat, wrinkly, old Slitherer. He was using his tail to stick a stone bowl through the bars.

"What is this place?" Treepalm asked, frightened by the giant snake in front of him.

"I told you. It's Grub's Grub. It's a tavern."

"Then why are we in cells?" asked Treepalm.

"All Slitherer taverns include prisons. We enjoy the fact that it's torture for you to listen to the sounds of freedom while imprisoned. Now take your grub."

Treepalm took the bowl to see that it was literally full of grubs - dirty, little, gray worms crawling all over each other. "Disgusting," he muttered.

Once Grub left, Treepalm began to hear muffled music and laughter. *It must be the tavern,* he thought. Just then he noticed another slit on another wall. Whoever was in there was saying, "Psst, kid. Come over here."

He did and saw a silhouette of an old, yellow dragon. In a scratchy voice, the dragon said, "My name is Sundrop. I think I know a way to escape."

* * *

"I have been here a very long time," said the old, yellow dragon. "I have studied every nook and cranny of my cell for some way - any way - to escape. I cannot believe I have not noticed this until now."

Sundrop held up a slightly cracked stone. "It was part of my wall. There is writing on the other side, a poem of some sort, possibly a way to escape."

"What does it say?" asked Treepalm.

Sundrop read out loud:

If you wish to leave this prison cell,
Pay attention. Sit down for a spell.
Abracadabra.
Here's a charm.
A Slitherer's pawn you'll be no more.
Out of reach.
Escape their net.
Each line, to the last letter, this riddle
You can't ignore.
Say it backwards to raise each bar.
Don't goof.

"Most likely, whoever wrote this was a prisoner themselves," said Sundrop.

"But why would a prisoner make it a riddle?" asked Treepalm.

"Every few days, Grub checks each cell. If he discovered this, he would probably think it was a bunch of gibberish written on a stone by a prisoner gone mad. If we are going to solve this riddle, we need to carefully study each line."

Sundrop moved closer to the slit in the wall. "The first line says: *If you wish to leave this prison cell, pay attention. Sit down for a spell.*"

"Well, we're definitely paying attention," noted Treepalm. "I suppose we should sit down."

"Wait a second," said Sundrop. "Spell could mean two things. Sit down for a while… or sit down to say a spell."

"That's it!" yelled Treepalm. "We have to sit down and say a spell. I bet the riddle will tell us what to say."

"Well," said Sundrop, "after all the next line is: *Abracadabra.*"

"Is that the spell?"

"Possibly. But it's too obvious. Let's keep studying this. The next line is: *Here is a charm…*"

"That tells us for sure it's a spell," said Treepalm. "I think the next line was: *A Slitherer's pawn you'll be no more.*"

"It's good to hear that," sighed Sundrop. "I've been a prisoner here for so long that I've lost count of the days."

"Eating only grubs?" asked Treepalm.

"You should smell my breath," said Sundrop. "Anyway… let's see… The next two lines are: *Out of reach. Escape their net*. And then: *Each line, to the last letter, this riddle…*"

"Now, that seems important," said Treepalm.

"Last letter... something about the last letter of each line," muttered Sundrop. "The next line is: *You can't ignore*. We can't ignore the last letter of each line!"

"Okay, what's next?"

Sundrop examined the stone brick. "*Say it backwards to raise each bar.*"

"That's it!" said Sundrop. "We have to sit down, figure out the last letter of each line, and then say it backwards."

"Wait!" interrupted Treepalm. "We forgot the last line: *Don't goof.*"

Sundrop sighed again. "I sure hope we don't."

* * *

"In order," said Treepalm, "the letters at the end of each line are... let's see... L-L-A-M-E-H-T-E-E-R-F. Backwards, that would be F-R-E-E-T-H-E-M-A-L-L."

Treepalm gave a curious look. "FREE THE MALL. FREE THE MALL? What's a mall?"

"I have no idea," said Sundrop. "Wait a minute... it's not FREE THE MALL!" He quickly sat down next to the bars of his cell. "It's... FREE THEM ALL!"

One by one, each bar on each cell glowed yellow and slowly rose, disappearing into the ceiling.

"Finally, I'm free. I can't wait to get the taste of grubs out of my mouth! Gather your friends, drah. We're going back to the surface!"

"The surface?" asked Treepalm. "We're underground?"

"I thought you knew," said Sundrop. "We're in the Slitherer tunnels."

* * *

When Treepalm had gathered the group, including their newest companion Fernpass, they met up with Sundrop outside the cells. There were no guards at the moment, to their relief.

"Good! You have gathered your friends. The good news is -- we're out of the cells. The bad news -- the only way out of the cell room is through the tavern."

"The tavern? How will we possibly get through there?" asked Merellia, nervously licking her Neomeon claws.

"I have a few tricks up my tail," grinned Sundrop.

They made their way down a hallway to a wooden door. Surprisingly, it wasn't locked.

"I'll go in first," said Sundrop.

They slowly nudged the door open and were hit by a blast of sound -- laughter, yelling, singing and fighting.

"I knew this was a tavern," said Treepalm, "but I didn't think it would be like this."

Most of the Slitherers were drunk. Some of them were wrestling. Others were belting out merry tunes.

"We have to be very quiet," said Sundrop. "We don't want to…"

"Burp!" Rift winced. "Sorry. Heh-heh. That was me. I may have… tried the grubs."

Now the entire tavern was looking at them. Then a Slitherer shouted, "Get them!" The tavern went into chaos, as the Slitherers charged at the dragons, the dragonfly and the Neomeon. Some knocked over tables. Others picked up random stones and threw them at the group. A few drew shiny, iron swords.

Suddenly, Sundrop's right front claw glowed bright yellow, and one of the swords leapt from a Slitherer's grasp and landed in Sundrop's claw. It, too, grew bright yellow. He thrust it into the nearest attacker's heart.

"That's for keeping me imprisoned!"

The attacker crumbled to ash. Sundrop then turned around and slashed another Slitherer through the neck. It, too, disintegrated into black ash.

"That's for forcing me to eat grubs."

He then stuck his sword into the floor. Blasts of orange light shot from it toward the remaining Slitherers in the room. Each of them erupted into flame and then ash.

"And that's," shouted Sundrop, "because you're just... plain... ugly!"

The group was gaping in awe. "H-how did you do that?" asked Treepalm.

"I'll tell you on the way. The exit is through those doors."

Across the tavern was a set of metal doors. As soon as they opened them, a terrible stench entered the room. They soon found out what it was. The doors opened into a dirt tunnel, far underground. Treepalm knew that snakes dug holes in the ground. He supposed it was the same with giant snakes. The floor was covered with lots of sludgy, green puddles. He realized that the puddles were emitting the stench. The companions were careful not to step into any of them.

Beesting was the first to ask Sundrop again. "How did you do that – that thing you did in the tavern?"

Sundrop grinned. "One simple word... magic."

* * *

As the group made its way through the tunnels, Sundrop explained. "A few dragons in the valley were born with special powers. Some don't know it yet. They are called Runekeepers."

"Runekeepers? Didn't that crazy fortuneteller say she was a Runekeeper?" asked Rift.

"You mean Gast?" said Sundrop. "She's a Poison Runekeeper. She's a very evil drai. No one knows where she came from. I myself am a Sun Runekeeper. I can control the might of the sun, although since we are so far underground, I can only perform weak runes."

"The thing you did in the tavern was weak?" asked Beesting.

"It was a simple levitation and heat rune."

"What do you mean by runes?" asked Flame.

"Basically," said Sundrop, "runes are spells. Each rune is represented by a certain symbol. When mastered, it can be used as a power. A Runekeeper's goal is to learn and master each rune. First, though, you have to find them."

"Find them how?" asked Jester

"Runes are all around us, invisibly drifting through the air. Runekeepers appear to be the only ones who can sense them."

"Wow," said Rift.

After a little while longer, the tunnel split into three directions.

"Which way do we go?" wondered Whitelizard.

"Wait a second!" said Treepalm. "The map I got from Dangle's antique store. I still have it! It's a map of the Slitherer tunnels!"

"Well then," said Sundrop. "Which way do we go?"

Treepalm squinted at the map. After making his best guess about where they might be, he said, "Um, the closest exit is… left."

For several hours, Treepalm led them through the tunnels, passing cobwebs, creepy statues with ruby eyes, and all sorts of rotting bones. At one point, they came to an open area with a sign stuck in the dirt that read, "SHEDDING GROUND." The room was filled with Slitherer skins, one on top of another.

"I recognize that skin," said Treepalm. "It was covering the tunnel where we found Jester. I knew that wasn't moss…"

"Slitherers often cover their tunnels with their skin. I find it disgusting," explained Sundrop.

Minutes later, they came to a locked door. Sundrop's claw glowed yellow and then so did the door, which slowly tilted open. "Simple unlock rune," Sundrop muttered. "Too bad it didn't work on my cell."

The room they entered was lit by candles on the floor. On a pedestal in the center of the room was…

"It can't be!" yelled Whitelizard. "It's… it's… it's…"

Sundrop smiled. "Ray's glasses!" His smile had turned to wonder. "I sense a new rune here - the Rune of Past Sight! It's floating near Treepalm. In fact… Treepalm's absorbing it! Treepalm! You have a rune! You're a Runekeeper!"

26: HE LIED

"Later, I will try to teach you how to use your powers. Now we must make our way out of these tunnels. I sense that the sun's presence is near."

Sundrop was correct. They soon came to a tunnel that rose toward the surface. The group ran to the exit. Seconds before they reached the top, two Slitherer guards blocked their path. They had sharp spears and blood-red eyes. One said, "You shall not pass. We will kill you and use your bones to scratch our backs!"

Then they attacked. One of them slashed at Whitelizard, who was protected by Sundrop's shield rune. The other swatted at Jester. He didn't have much luck. Sundrop sent blasts of light at both of them, and they fell to the ground. He turned to his companions.

"After you," he told the group.

"No," said Treepalm. "After you."

Sundrop raised his chin high and, for the first time in years, walked out into the bright sunlight.

As soon as Treepalm stepped on the surface, he smelled blood. Merellia was the first to spot the trail of blood. It led behind a wide tree. Chained to the back of it was a red drah, looking old and weak.

"Um, hello?" said Treepalm.

The dragon turned his head. "Can you help me?" he croaked.

"Of course. What's your name?"

In a whisper, the dragon said, "Rorwain."

* * *

"You killed my father!" Treepalm shouted.

"I did no such thing."

"Then who did?"

Rorwain clenched his teeth and balled his claw into a fist. "Black."

Flame spoke to his father with anger and confusion in his voice. "My brother may be brutish, but he would not lie. I'm sure it's you. I... I am sure... it... was... you."

"Rage hypnotized you to believe that I murdered Rohawk. You must remember. Remember... Remember!"

Flame looked confused for a moment. Then he suddenly blinked and his eyes brightened. "I do remember now."

"Rage works for Black," said Rorwain. "He plans to win the Tournament of Kings, get the huge pile of prey and give it to the Slitherers. In return, the Slitherers would join Black's growing army. Black would be almost unstoppable. I am the only one who knows this. Rage, my evil son, chained me to this tree and set you up to be captured."

Flame paced for several minutes, while the others just watched in silence. Finally, he spoke. "We have to stop him. But how?"

"I know a way," said Rift. "As we were heading to Dangle's, I heard other dragons talking about how Streakedegg was hurt in the strength tournament. So he can't do the last event, the hunting tournament. If one of us volunteered to take his place and win, perhaps Rage would lose the Tournament of Kings."

"I'll go," said Flame. "He's my brother. But now, he's my enemy."

"Sundrop," said Beesting, "can you free Rorwain?"

"Of course, it'll only take a couple of unlock runes and careful metal melt runes."

"Good," said Flame. "I'm heading to the hunting tournament.

"Are you sure you want to do this?" asked Treepalm.

"Yes. I'm sure."

Rorwain looked at Flame and smiled. "Good luck, my son."

* * *

Only ten minutes later, Flame stood next to nine other competitors at the Hunting Grounds. Rage eyed him and whispered, "You cannot beat me, brother. Run while you can."

"Don't be too sure," Flame snarled. They were in the eastern section of Sun Woods. *Prey is plentiful here,* thought Flame. *Hopefully, I can get a stroke of luck.*

And then, the tournament began. Rage raced off. Flame quickly followed. Luckily, Flame immediately smelled a snake, resting by the roots of a tree. He was able to quickly kill it. *I've had enough snakes for one day,* he thought.

He could see, in the distance, that Rage had already caught a squirrel. Flame raced over there, thinking there may be more. He flew up to a strong branch near the top of a tall tree and spotted two squirrels. *What great luck!*

After catching the squirrels, Flame dove back down to where Rage was, hoping to check on his progress. Rage had already snagged two mice and a snake.

Flame came too close, and Rage turned around. "Flee, brother. You have no chance of succeeding."

Flame didn't budge. His own brother lunged at him and pinned him to the ground. "I… said… flee!"

Flame fought his way free and ran in the opposite direction. After a little while, he stumbled upon a mouse. Flame expertly caught it before it knew what was happening. After another ten minutes, he thought, *I better check on how Rage is doing. This time I'll be more careful.*

He once again had great luck. Rage hadn't found any more prey. As soon as he saw this, Flame quickly hurried into the forest to catch more. Soon Flame had collected a total of seven prey. He went back to Rage. He had seven, too! Flame wasn't as cautious this time, and Rage saw him. "Stay away, brother. I am about to win."

Flame's brother was eyeing a raven on a low branch. "Not if I win first," said Flame.

They both flew at the raven at the same time and crashed into each other in midair. The bird flew away before either of them could catch it.

"You fool!" Rage shouted at his brother.

Just then, they both heard a rustle in a nearby shrub, and a rabbit poked its head out. The two brothers looked at the animal and then at each other.

"It's mine," whispered Rage. But Flame was too fast. The rabbit was in his teeth.

Rage grabbed the other side with his strong jaw. Flame could barely hold on. The only thing that gave him strength was one thought: *He lied to me.*

Unexpectedly, and unbelievably, Flame somehow pulled the prey out of Rage's teeth. "No! It's mine!" he said.

They heard a loud horn. The tournament had ended. They then heard a voice from above them. It shouted, "Flame wins by a hare!"

PART 4:
THE FOURTH AGE

27: GENERATIONS

"So Flame grew up to be a very important member of our tribe, and Rage's plot was discovered. As punishment, Rage was exiled, sent to live out the rest of his days in a cave on the outskirts of our territory."

A young red drai raised her tail. "Excuse me, Miss Tailtinge."

"Yes?"

"Did this story really take place nine hundred thirty-four years ago?"

"Yes. In fact, there were barely one hundred dragons in the valley at that time."

"That's absurd!" shouted a slightly older red drah. "How was this story preserved?"

"Knowers like me," said Miss Tailtinge. "Now, back to the story… Rage has died, obviously. After all, only the original dragon leaders are still living from that age. Well, all but one, of course. Flame and his group are legends now. Merellia is a symbol of hope within the Neomeons. Dragonflies have written songs about Jester Mountebank. But let's get back to Rage. Some claim that his spirit still lingers, hunting more prey."

"What do you think, Miss Tailtinge?" asked the drai.

"I think there's a lot of bad in Dragon Valley that still lingers."

* * *

"Welcome, Runekeepers, to Runekeeper Keep, founded by the legendary Treepalm!" The group of new runekeepers gaped at the large stone fort in front of them. It had long, vertical windows and shiny, green banners.

"I am the current Head Dragon. In fact, I am the 37th great-granddaughter of Treepalm, himself. My name is Springseeker, and I will be getting you acquainted with Runekeeper Keep. Treepalm, known as the father of Runekeeper Keep, with the help of Sundrop, known as the grandfather of Runekeeper Keep, built the fort you see before you for the few runekeepers in the valley at that time. It has now expanded into the Keep you see today. I'm sure several of you are descendants of Treepalm and his mate, Puddlejump. Some of you already have the ability to see into the past, a trait inherited from Treepalm. I have heard that a few of you even have the ability to talk with people from the past. That's a very special power."

Springseeker began to walk among the young dragons. "I'm curious, if you could talk with someone from the past, with whom would you speak?"

"I'd speak with Sundrop," said a young green drah. "I heard he could perform some amazing runes."

"I'd speak with the Neomeon, Azalea. I've always wanted to talk with her about the medicine she developed," said a white drai.

There was a pause for a moment until a small, yellow drah spoke up. "I'd talk with Ray."

The group gasped. Springseeker said what the others were thinking. "You can't talk with a god."

* * *

Yellow, now much larger and wiser, strode through Sun Woods. *The valley seems so much smaller than it did when I first arrived,* she thought. Yellow was near the place where the she and the other dragons had raced to the small redwood tree so long ago. But now it was enormous. Its bark was hard and thick, its trunk round and wide. Its branches stretched out like it was showing its claws.

Yellow distinctly remembered that first race involving the original five dragons. She also remembered that Blue couldn't participate because he couldn't fly. Blue's tribe was having trouble with Black – even more trouble than usual.

War was inevitable.

* * *

"We can't wait here like lazy scaletails," yelled General Splash. "We must defend ourselves!"

"Indeed, I feel the same way you do," said Blue. "But we have to hold our attack until we have reinforcements from the other tribes."

Just then, a young blue dragon charged into the cave. "A large army of fireflies and bats are descending on our territory!"

"Scratch that," said Blue to his general. "Battle it is."

* * *

In one of the farthest outposts of the blue tribe were a group of dracos and their parents. One of the smaller dracos, a little drai named Petalswim, asked her mother, "Why are we hiding? I want Daddy."

"Daddy's a battle dragon, dear. He has to do his job."

"Why is Daddy fighting Black, Mommy?" the innocent draco asked.

"Well…" said the mother, "in the middle of our lake, Black has an island…"

"Shadow Island! Some older drahs said that's where shadow spirits nibble your claws off!"

"Nonsense," said the mother. "Don't listen to those pesky drahs. Anyway, Black has been demanding more of the lake near the island, nearly half of our territory."

"Black is a bad dragon," said Petalswim.

"Yes, a very bad dragon."

* * *

In the snowy wilderness on the mountain of the white tribe, Red stood shivering and staring at a large, five-foot-in-diameter, stone half-circle with markings all over the top that were runes of frost.

"White was a great leader before he died," said a voice from behind her.

Red whipped around. "Oh, it's you, Whitelizard. You startled me."

"You, most of all, should know to call me by my full name – Whitelizard the 28th."

"That is no way to talk to a leader," Red snapped, "even if you are a leader yourself."

"I'm sorry, Red. I know you've been depressed since White's death so long ago. I know you visit his shrine every week. "

"Why did White have to eat that snake?" Red asked, mostly to herself.

"Why did Black have to poison the snake?" Whitelizard replied. There was a moment of silence. "I know what will make you feel better, Red – a *syonim.*"

A syonim was a word for a food the white dragons had created. Since they spent so much time with their chill orbs over the years, evolution had made the orbs now a part of them. Just by breathing a certain way, they could freeze objects. They made syonims by scooping sap from a tree and freezing it. It tasted sweet and made your body feel warm.

"Thanks," said Red, taking the treat from Whitelizard the 28th. Red felt a little warmer and happier, but not by much. White was still gone.

* * *

"There are not enough dragons for the revolt," said the serious, yet young, purple drah.

"Yes, too many purple dragons support Black."

Just then, another purple drah walked in. "Twig, Maple, what is this about?"

"Hello, Cloudhopper, we've noticed that you no longer seem to support Black," said Twig.

Cloudhopper was silent, and then... "Will I be punished?"

"No," said Maple. "You may have noticed that recently there has been a division in our tribe."

The drah nodded, as Twig continued the thought. "Some support Black. Others don't."

"We don't," said Maple. "One-third of the tribe doesn't. We're planning a revolt. Will you join?"

Cloudhopper thought for a moment, then bared his teeth in a smile. "Of course."

*   *   *

Deep in the halls of the Neomeon Mountains, Xillar, chief Neomeon storyteller (basically, a Neomeon knower) told a small group of mountain lion cubs a tale of long ago.

"Hundreds of years ago, when we were split into three groups instead of two… Do you cubs know what the three groups were?"

The cubs shook their heads. "Do any of their parents teach them about history?" he muttered. "Their names were the Lios Neos or light Neomeons, who were against Black and lived in Mount Leo… the Svart Neos or dark Neomeons, who followed Black to gain riches and lived in Echo Mountain… and the Caivat, who simply didn't want war. They lived on Aexis Peak."

"Here!" squeaked one of the cubs.

"Yes, they lived in this very mountain. Let's get back to the story, though. Back then, there were terrible battles among the factions. But eventually, the Lios Neos and the Caivat negotiated a treaty. They would join together and form the Caios Neos and promised to use less brutal ways to settle their differences. That treaty - the Treaty of Diplomacy - hangs in this very hall. So now we are two groups - the Svart Neos and the Caios Neos. Perhaps one day, we will join together as one group once again. But that day has not arrived."

The young cubs pounded the ground with their feet, the Neomeon way of clapping. One cub demanded, "We want another!"

"I'm sorry," said Xillar. "You can come back tomorrow."

The cubs began to leave the room. As soon as they were gone, a large, brown Neomeon stepped from the shadows toward Xillar. "Ah, King Darnox. I wasn't aware you were watching."

"You did well," said the king. "It is important to teach cubs about the wrongs of joining Black's army - or our tribe will split once more."

"You look worried, my king," said Xillar.

"I am."

* * *

In the center of the Great Forest, hanging from a tree, was a large, golden ball of sorts. Dragons without a sharp eye might mistake it for a beehive while they walked on the forest floor. But it glowed brightly and was too large to be a beehive. No, it was one of five dragonfly message centers around the valley.

Inside, there was action everywhere. Dragonflies of every color flew around, either leaving the center to deliver a message or returning to the center after delivering one. One of the top messengers, Vine Mountebank, the 1,542nd great-grandson of Jester Mountebank himself, had just returned from delivering and reading a message.

"Sorry, Vine, I have one more for you," said a large, blue dragonfly, holding a tiny, balled-up message. "It's from Yellow to… can this be true?"

"To whom?" asked Vine.

"To Black." Looking up, he added, "Be careful."

"Don't worry," said Vine. "I'll be just fine."

* * *

Black lounged lazily on his new throne. *It'll take some getting used to,* he thought, *although I make my servants craft me a new throne every week.*

"A dragonfly has a message for you, Lord Black," said a bat.

"Let him in," Black demanded.

Vine quickly flew in, as Black asked, "What is it, you winged slug?"

"It... it's a message from Yellow, your Lordy-majestery-scariness..." Vine gulped, cleared his throat and held up the unrolled message to his tiny eyes. "You will not win, Black. I am sending reinforcements to aid the blue tribe. I suggest you hold off your attacks." Vine looked up, an odd expression of both horror and amusement on his face. "Th-that's all, sir," he stuttered.

Black shouted, "That frog-munching smoke-breather." In an instant, he grabbed the poor dragonfly from mid air and squished him in his grasp. There would be no 1,543rd generation of Mountebanks.

28: PROGRESS

"The bats are overwhelming us, Blue!" yelled General Splash in the midst of battle.

Blue was swimming around, surveying the fighting. *We still have a small advantage,* he thought. *We're in the water. It will be harder for them to get to us all.* The blue dragons were greatly outnumbered, though. Many lifeless bodies floated on the water's surface. For the blue tribe, it wasn't a battle to win. It was a battle to survive.

Just then, to Blue's surprise, a strong-looking she-bat lunged at his scarred shoulder. Blue shouted in pain. *She must be a general,* Blue thought. Then Blue recognized her. She was General Poisonfang. Some dragons called her Madame Fang. She was one of the best fighters in Black's army, known for coating her fangs with poison.

Blue was dazed. His eyes were blurry. The world turned around him. He saw strange flashes of color and sound, and they began to grow dimmer…

"Hey, Madame Fart! Over here!"

Blue barely made out his mate Yellow's face… and her army behind her. He smiled. She smiled back and then made a grand swipe at Madame Fang, knocking her head clean off.

Another bat, General Pokewing, saw Poisonfang's death and yelled, "Retreat! Retreat!" The army quickly did so.

Once Black's legions left, Yellow took a long look at Blue's injury. "It's not bad, Blue. You'll live.... forever, I hope."

"Thank you for saving me and my tribe," said Blue, as he looked around sadly. "Or what's left of it."

"You're very welcome," she said. "I've been thinking... I think you should evacuate your territory. It's safe in mine at the moment. You know the lake I have in my territory? Your tribe can live there for now. It's much smaller, but it will work."

"After more than nine centuries of being mates," said Blue, "we will finally share a territory."

* * *

"I'm telling you," said Maple to Twig, "we don't have enough rebels to... rebel."

"There must be something we can do!"

"We will, but not today. Our best option is to escape Black's territory with as many purple dragons as we can and head to Yellow's territory. We'll explain who we are, and it will be easier to start an army."

Twig sighed. "If we must."

"Steamsnort!" Maple called. A very young purple drah ran into the cave and tripped over a small bump. Steamsnort was, in a way, their second in command. Not officially, though. Nothing in the Purple Rebellion was official. Steamsnort took his job seriously, and he had actually proven to be quite useful, but he was also very clumsy.

After Steamsnort picked himself up, Maple and Twig stared at him with serious expressions. Twig spoke. "This is very important, Lieutenant Steam, we need to gather all of the tribe members who would support a rebellion. We leave in an hour."

Steamsnort nodded.

* * *

An hour later, the purple rebels stood at the edge of Black's territory. "We are going to divide into two factions. I will lead half of our group through Green's territory to Yellow's," said Maple. "Twig will lead the other half through white territory and Red's territory, eventually meeting up with us in Yellow's. That way, if one group is discovered, the other can still make it."

"Are there any questions?" asked Twig.

Not a single dragon raised a tail.

* * *

Twig's group slowly climbed the steep slopes of the white tribe's mountain. Walking briskly because it was too cold to fly, they were quickly coated with frost.

"I dislike this cold," stated Lieutenant Steam.

"As do I," Twig replied.

Unbeknownst to them, there was a white drah, a scout, patrolling the border of Black's territory. He had spotted them as soon as they entered the white dragons' region. *We're under attack,* he thought. *I must warn Whitelizard.* So he ran as fast as his dragon legs would take him. (He would have liked to have flown, but he had volunteered for scout duty despite an injured wing.) He ran so quickly he barely left a claw print in the snow. Not ten minutes later, he arrived at Whitelizard's cavern.

As soon as the scout spoke, Whitelizard called for his best generals. "Assemble the battle dragons. We are under attack by the purple tribe!"

* * *

"Is that mountain moving?" asked Steamsnort.

"Don't be absurd," said Twig. But it was moving, very slightly, almost as if it were shivering. Twig squinted. "What..."

The white dragons charged. It was a large army, around 100 battle dragons. They were about to reach the purple group when Twig shouted, "Stop!"

Surprised, the first line of the white army stopped in its tracks, causing the second line to bump into them. The rest of the rows followed. "Clumsy army," Whitelizard muttered. "We have to work on that." He then shouted, "Why do you come here?"

Twig walked alone toward Whitelizard, who met him halfway. Twig explained who they were, and then Whitelizard said, "You won't last long in our cold territory. My tribe will escort you to Yellow."

* * *

In the dark of night, a faint noise awoke Green. She strode out of her cave. The noise grew slightly louder. It was coming from the ground. It sounded like a symphony of hissing. *Wait a second. Hissing...*

The ground next to her exploded in a shower of dirt. It was a Slitherer raid! At least 30 Slitherers, their tails armed with blood-rusted iron swords and leather slingshots loaded with spiked iron balls.

"Slitherer attack!" Green yelled.

The green dragons were swift, but the Slitherers had the element of surprise, which gave them quite an advantage. The dragons who managed to arrive to defend the area began with a ground battle. It didn't prove to work very well.

The Slitherers were flexible and fast with their swords. They were also extremely good at dodging attacks. Soon many dragons tried diving from the sky. That didn't work well either. The Slitherers aimed their slingshots at the dragons' wings. A number of dragons fell to the ground, either dead or severely injured. It was no use. They were greatly outmatched.

Ray, please help us, Green thought.

That was when Maple and her faction of dragons appeared. The darkness hid their purple scales, and they swooped down to strike the group of Slitherers, who didn't know what hit them. Half of the group was killed almost immediately. But they weren't done fighting yet.

Just then, Green felt a nip on her ankle. She looked down. It was a snake, two feet tall, one-fourth the size of a normal Slitherer. It was the Slitherer leader – Sargoth the Small. The magic had entered him the wrong way, so he hadn't grown bigger. But he had still become smarter – so smart that he had emerged as the Slitherer leader. In fact, he had been the Slitherer leader almost as long as Green had led her dragons.

As Sargoth sliced at Green's ankles, she tried to claw at him. But he moved faster than she expected. Green flapped her wings and rose into the night sky. Sargoth raised his tiny sword. "You will be crushed!"

Green dropped to the ground with an enormous thud – right on top of the Slitherer leader.

"No," she said. "You will."

The Slitherers retreated into the Great Forest. Maple went to Green and explained who they were, and Green was grateful. "They are leaderless for now, but they might return. We will come with you to Yellow's territory. There we can regroup."

* * *

"Rulebender, by now you must know the ways of the Grizzclaw!"

"I am sorry, Father, but I am curious about the world outside of our small territory."

"Son, we Grizzclaw value our privacy and our neutrality. Remember that."

Rulebender hesitated. "Yes, Father."

Then another Grizzclaw arrived breathlessly. "Leader," he told Rulebender's father, who was known as Swiftwing because he was the best flyer among the flying bears. "Slitherer's are approaching fast! They have weapons!"

"Slitherers? Here? Why would they be attacking us?" He paused for a moment. "Send the army!"

"Yes, sir."

The Slitherers may have taken the green dragons by surprise, but not the Grizzclaw. Quickly, the bears gained the upper… claw. The Slitherers were already weakened by their battle with the green and purple dragons. They hadn't meant to retreat into Grizzclaw territory. In the middle of the battle, the green and purple dragons arrived, as they were on their way to Yellow's territory. Soon, the few remaining Slitherers, including Grit, Sargoth's second-in-command, now their leader, were surrounded.

"There is no escape," said Green.

Grit then spoke in a strong, powerful voice. "Oh yes there is. The Slitherers burrowed into the ground in the blink of an eye. After they had left, Green and Swiftwing strode up to each other.

"We still prefer to stay out of Dragon Valley's conflicts, but we thank you," said Swiftwing. "It is good to have friends."

* * *

The red dragon patrol flew swiftly above the heat of the high desert. Nothing much was usually spotted during patrols, but better safe than sorry. They saw something that day, though. At first, they thought it was a strange whitish-purple cloud. As it drew nearer, they realized what it really was – the white and purple dragons slowly making their way through the scorching skies above The Desert.

The white dragons were having an especially hard time. Their scales were easily burned, and they were slow in heat. The two-colored cloud landed, and the red patrol did the same. General Ash, leading the patrol, stepped forward to speak with Whitelizard.

"Whitelizard, old friend, how have you been?"

"I've been fine, Ash."

"What brings you here?"

Whitelizard explained to the general what they were doing.

"I should report this to Red," said Ash. "While you are waiting, you and your group can rest by Fire Lake.

It's only a bit north. Don't be deceived by the name. It will cool you down. I'll be back in an hour or two."

Without another word, the patrol flew off.

*   *   *

General Ash was always a little worried before reporting to Red, who had kept to the shadows in recent years, having never quite overcome the loss of White. When Ash stepped in, Red was curled in a corner, facing the cave wall.

"Um, Red, I have an important report to give you."

"Tell me quickly," she murmured.

"It seems a large section of purple dragons are rebelling against Black. They are traveling to Yellow's territory to build a larger army. The white tribe is going with them. Should we join them?"

Red paused, staring into a shallow pool of water in her cave. She saw a great dragon looking back at her. She knew what she had to do. "It seems that the final struggle for Dragon Valley is upon us. Yes, we will go. May Ray help us."

29: BATTLE PLANS

Yellow was resting in her cave in a hillside, musing about the future. A yellow dragonfly flew in.

"Yellow! We dragonflies have spotted many green dragons following a small group of purple dragons and coming this way!"

Yellow rose to her feet. "Purple dragons? What would they want here?"

"I don't know," said the dragonfly.

"Blue and I will go and see them," said Yellow. "I'm sure there is a reason."

Yellow stepped outside, and there they were, swiftly flying toward her, the sun reflecting off their scales. That's when Blue arrived.

"My blue dragonfly messenger has seen a cluster of white, red and purple dragons coming our way from the east!" Blue glanced where Yellow was looking and saw the green and purple dragons. "What is going on?"

That's when they saw the Neomeons quickly striding toward them from the southeast.

* * *

Yellow stood with many leaders – Red, Blue, Green, Whitelizard, Maple and Twig, and the Neomeon king Darnox. First, Yellow asked Maple and Twig why they had come, and they explained about the rebellion. Then Green told Yellow about the Slitherer raid.

"That could become a problem," said Red.

Finally, Yellow asked King Darnox, "Now what brings you here to my territory?"

"I fear that if Black continues to rise in power, our Neomeon kingdom may split once again." The king lowered his head. "That must not happen."

"It won't," said Yellow.

Just then, a dragonfly burst in. "Make way for the Royal Highness Larwar - King of the Dragonflies!"

A handsome, young dragonfly with a long golden sword (long for dragonflies, anyway) appeared. "I come because one of our best messengers, Vine Mountebank, has been murdered by Black. This has happened countless times, almost every time a messenger is sent to that vicious, black beast. I cannot allow this to happen any longer."

"Please, join our meeting, King Larwar. We were just talking about Black," said Yellow.

"I say we attack," said Twig, as Larwar joined the circle.

That one remark caused much arguing and shouting.

"Silence!" yelled Yellow. "I agree with Twig. We knew this day would come. We have waited much too long. I would like for us to all agree, however. So I ask you all, is it time?"

Slowly, each leader nodded.

King Larwar held his sword to the sky. "Then let us make battle plans!"

* * *

At the entrance to a nearby cave, a dragon named Darkroot stood in front of a troop of battle dragons. Darkroot had gray scales. He was one of the few dragons who did. Darkroot used to be yellow, but one day, when he was a draco, he wandered into the wilderness. He was gone from his tribe for too long, and his scales turned gray. But in the wilderness, he had to fend for himself and survive, so he returned as one of the best battle dragons alive. Darkroot quickly became Yellow's general, training young battle dragons. As soon as he found out there was to be a battle, he trained as many as he could to the best of his ability.

War would soon be upon them.

* * *

"We cannot live in solitude forever!" a Grizzclaw shouted.

"I understand your point," said another. "But it is safer and wiser to stay out of conflicts."

The leader of the Grizzclaw, Swiftwing, stepped forward. "A war is brewing. We all know that. We have a choice. Do we join the fight or hide in terror?"

"Are you actually suggesting we fight?" said an older Grizzclaw.

"I am only stating our choices."

"We are not hiding in terror," said the older bear. "We are simply keeping ourselves safe."

Determination showed in Swiftwing's eyes. "The only way to defeat danger... is to be dangerous ourselves."

* * *

"Summon my generals!" Black demanded.

"Yes, sir," a guard bat replied.

Soon Black was staring into the eyes of his four generals - Pokewing the bat, King Gorcaak the firefly, Crunch the Svart Neomeon… and Purple. Technically, Purple was a dragon leader. But since Black had control over the purple tribe, she became his general.

"My spies," Black began, "have told me that our enemies are planning to attack."

"Then I suggest we attack first," said King Gorcaak.

"I second that," said General Pokewing.

"As do I," said Crunch.

Black and the three generals turned to purple. "Well?" said Black.

Purple simply nodded her head.

Pokewing immediately started talking about battle plans. "I suggest we attack from the west. We will be faster that way."

Black agreed. "They will have a nasty surprise if we go through Green's territory. We will be weakened if we go through the icy cold of the white territory and the blazing heat of the red region. We must not show weakness in war."

* * *

Yellow sat face to face with Blue. "My spies tell me that Black plans to attack," she explained.

"Are you saying we should attack first?"

"Yes. Are the battle dragons, Neomeons and dragonflies prepared?"

"General Darkroot trained them well."

"Good. Darkroot has never failed me."

Blue smiled. "Are you worried?" he asked.

"Well, yes. This battle could affect the course of Dragon Valley's history… Can we get back to battle plans, though?"

"Of course. I say we go through Green's territory. We'll be faster that way."

"Then we shall leave for battle immediately."

* * *

While Black's army marched north, Yellow's army marched south (the Neomeons on each side would not have been able to keep up if they flew). As they marched through the grassy fields of Yellow's territory, Red surveyed their numbers. She counted around 600 dragons, 200 Neomeons, 1,000 dragonflies - nearly 1,800 soldiers in all. Red then smiled.

We can win, she thought.

An hour later, they came to a flat field and Green's territory. Bordering one side of the field was the Great Forest. That's when it happened. There was a rustling in the bushes on the other side of the field, and Black stepped out. His scales were as dark as ever, and he stood even a bit taller than Yellow. He smirked at her. Then his army emerged behind him - almost 3,000 soldiers including some 200 purple dragons.

Suddenly, Black's attention turned to something else. Yellow followed his gaze. Her eyes landed on a pile of bones, yellowed with age. They were cracked and crumbled. The sun seemed to reflect upon them through the leaves of two young birch trees.

The bones were human. The bones… were Ray's.

Black's smirk grew just a bit larger.

30: THE BATTLE OF THE BONES

The great battle forever would be known by dragonkind as the Battle of the Bones. It started with a stare down. Black and Yellow glared at each other. Black then spoke. "Are you prepared, Yellow?"

"I have been for almost a thousand years."

The armies charged at each other and collided in a chorus of shouts, swipes and groans. High above the chaos, two swarms of flying bugs hovered. King Larwar of the dragonflies held his long, golden sword. Many dragonflies in the future claimed it shone fiercer and brighter than the very sun. King Gorcaak of the fireflies held a blood red scabbard sharper than a dragon tooth.

It was a tradition among dragonflies and fireflies to have their leaders face off before a battle to cause confusion for the group whose leader dies. Confusion was a powerful weapon.

"If I die, may I die with glory!" yelled Larwar.

Their swords clashed -- a tiny *thwack* to human ears, but a sharp *twang* to dragonflies. Their swords clashed many times over. They twisted and twirled in the air. Some might call it graceful... if each wasn't trying to slice the other's head off.

The dragonfly king held his sword to the sun, momentarily blinding his foe. This was his chance. He plunged his sword into the firefly's heart, but Gorcaak did the same to Larwar. They both fell from the air, each one's weapons still protruding from the other's body.

They had brought confusion, but also anger and sorrow - deep sorrow. Both had fallen with glory.

* * *

On the ground, Neomeons fought with tooth and claw, moving so quickly that they looked like flashes of brown and tan. King Darnox of the Caios Neos fought bravely in the middle of the battlefield, as more and more Svart Neos attacked him. He killed them all, but was severely injured. The king had a deep cut on his foreleg. He tried to limp away, but he was too slow. A group of Svart were after him.

Busy amid the confusion and chaos, nobody noticed King Darnox's predicament, except Darnox's general, General Rastlen, who ran over to defend his king. It was a large group of attackers, around a dozen. All were much larger than Rastlen, who was very small. He had barely grown as a cub. Little did his attackers know, that was his advantage.

"Oh, look. It's a little cub!" one laughed. "Do you want some milk, little one?"

"No, said Rastlen. "I want you dead."

He swiftly ran at them, taking all by surprise. He scratched and bit his way to success. Within moments, six of them lay dead.

But Rastlen was exhausted, and King Darnox was injured, and there were still six bloodthirsty attackers remaining.

The general turned to his king. "Is this the end?"

"It is what it is," Darnox replied.

But just then, the sky was darkened by flying figures that they first thought to be dragons. Rastlen squinted and realized who they were.

"Grizzclaw!" he shouted. "But… which side are they on?"

He soon learned the answer. Ten of them landed between the attacking Svart Neos and the injured king. They quickly wiped out the attackers with a few swift swipes of their razor-sharp claws.

One of the Grizzclaw nodded toward King Darnox and flew off, followed by his companions, to aid in other parts of the battle.

Rastlen walked up to one of the attackers, who was still barely alive. "I'll have that milk now," he whispered.

* * *

Yellow and the other dragons had set up a small, temporary camp north of the battle. She was leading another meeting. King Larwar's son, Prince Hultark, rushed to Yellow. "My father, the king! He's… dead," the prince whispered.

Yellow was shocked. "He's dead? That's horrible. You must go back to the dragonflies and lead them. You are now the king – all hail King Hultark!"

"Th-thank you," the new king stuttered. "I should leave then. Farewell!"

King Hultark flew into the sky to lead his troops.

"Now," said Yellow, "King Darnox, how is your leg?"

"It… is fine."

Yellow gave it a look. "I wouldn't say that. I'm surprised you can move. You are not fit for battle.

General Rastlen will lead your army. You have done your part, Darnox. Take a rest."

The Neomeon king nodded. "Very well."

Red suddenly spoke. "Yellow, I have a battle report."

"Please, tell us."

"The Caios Neos have the upper claw. They have outnumbered the Svart and are most likely going to succeed."

"That's wonderful," said Yellow. But Red was frowning. "What's the bad news?"

"The dragonflies are losing. Hopefully, Hultark will reverse their fortunes. Also, no one can get close to hurting Black without being killed." Red straightened. "One of us has to face him."

"Then face him I shall," Yellow shouted. "But first, Green, my daughter, I must talk to you alone."

* * *

Yellow, Green and another green drah named Shimmer stood in a quiet cave, the sounds of distant battle echoing through its walls.

"Are you prepared?" Green asked.

"As prepared as I could be," Shimmer replied, though he was clearly nervous.

Yellow nodded. "Then you may proceed, runekeeper."

Shimmer tightly closed his eyes, concentrating on only his breathing, and began whispering a magical rune that only he could hear. Suddenly, a misty, gray smoke began to fill the room. It swirled, faster and faster, and collected in a single spot in front of the dragons. Then a figure emerged. It had two legs and two arms, a bald head fringed with gray hair. It was a man. He wore glasses. It was the man who had created it all.

Yellow whispered, stunned and delighted, "Ray!"

"Yellow? Is that you? You're huge! What's going on? Where am I?"

"You're… in the future. Dragon Valley's future."

"That's impossible!" said Ray. "How can it be?"

"I'm afraid it's too complicated to explain," said Yellow, "and we don't have much time…."

Ray interrupted, looking at the other two dragons. "And Green! You were small when I last saw you, when you saved me from that bear."

"I am a leader now," said Green proudly. "I have been for nearly nine hundred years."

"Nine hundred? Years? Leader of… what?"

"The green tribe," she responded. "Many hundreds of dragons now occupy the valley."

"Tribes? There are tribes? Last I recall, there were only six dragons - Red, White, Yellow, Blue, baby Green… and Black."

"Yes," said Yellow. "about Black…"

"We only have seconds remaining," Shimmer interrupted.

"You created Black, just like you are responsible for creating all of us…"

"Not every creation can be successful," said Ray. "Black is… different."

"How do you know?" asked Green.

"I knew from the second I brought him to life."

"He has become too powerful, too strong, too wicked," said Yellow. "Dragon Valley cannot survive if Black does…"

Ray's figure began to fade into smoke again. But before he vanished completely, the dragons heard nine final words. "I created life, but only you can destroy it."

* * *

Yellow returned to the dragon leaders. "Let us leave for battle."

From a distance, all could see the silhouettes of four large, old dragons – Yellow, Red, Green, and Whitelizard – flying high in the sky. Blue swiftly followed on foot.

"Black is closely guarded," said Red. "We will have to get through his defenses."

Yellow nodded. "To battle!" she cried, as she sped headlong into the deadly brawl and quickly knocked a purple drah from the air. Red clawed at another soldier's face. Green kicked a bat out of existence, while Whitelizard used his tail to club seven bats into oblivion.

Yellow looked toward the ground, where Blue was plowing forward, allowing nothing to get in his way. Suddenly, he stopped. Above him, hovered a shadow. Blue looked up to see Black killing anyone in his path and speeding downward with his claws outstretched. But just before Black landed on Blue, something collided with him, knocking him to the ground. Black rose to his feet. Yellow stood in front of him.

Black only laughed. "Nice to see you, Yellow. How have you been doing?"

"Do not mock me, Black. You know what we must do."

"Let's get on with it then."

The fight began, as the two dragons took to the air. Yellow was the first to attack. She jumped on top of

Black, but he quickly swerved away. She tried again. But he dodged. This time, she almost fell out of the evening's scarlet sky. *How can I do this?* she thought.

That's when Black attacked. He leapt onto her, and she fell toward the ground below with Black on top of her, digging his claws deep into her scales. Yellow fell for what seemed like forever. Jumbles of color whipped past her. She then hit the ground with a hard *THUMP*, as Black rolled alongside her. Yellow couldn't move. She could barely stay conscious.

Black stepped forward to deliver the killing blow. *This is it,* thought Yellow. *Dragon Valley is lost.* But the pain never came. Yellow looked up to see a very large purple drai standing near her.

"Ah, Purple, you have come to see Yellow's demise?" Black grinned.

"No," said Purple. "I have come to see yours."

It happened fast. Purple kicked Black in the gut and sent him flying into a tree. He quickly pulled himself together and came back to attack. Purple was ready. As he lunged to bite her, she grabbed hold of his neck and squeezed.

"Why, Purple?" Black gurgled. "Why?"

"I had a change of heart," Purple replied, and she squeezed harder.

"No… No!!!!"

Black dropped… dead.

"Purple…" Yellow whispered.

"I know, Yellow. You are very angry with me for what I have done for all these years, for betraying the dragons, for betraying my parents. I am deeply sorry. I will receive any punishment you inflict upon me."

"What I was going to say, Purple, was... you're not you."

"I agree. This was very... unexpected."

"No," said Yellow. "I mean your scales."

Yellow was right. Purple's scales had changed.

"Purple," said Yellow. "You have become Pink."

Pink looked at herself, amazed. "I... I... I can't believe this."

"We can," said Red from behind her. "And so would your father, if he still were alive. You are my true daughter."

Pink turned around to see that all of the leaders had arrived. The battle had been won. They were all kneeling at her feet. Yellow stood up, then knelt herself. Then she spoke.

"Pink, you are the dragon who has been hidden in Purple all these years. You are what should have been. We kneel to you, Pink. You... are one of us."

* * *

The days that followed were peaceful and joyous in the valley. After the battle, the dragons had many feasts and celebrations. Pink gained control of Black's old territory and became leader of the purple rebels. Twig and Maple became her trusted generals, although there was little need for fighting dragons anymore. Evil was vanquished forever. Or so they thought.

But hidden in a small cave on Shadow Island was one black egg. It was just beginning to crack.

GLOSSARY

Ash (male): red dragon of the Fourth Age, Red's general

Azalea (female): Neomeon, born at the end of the Third Age; developed an important medicine

Back-kick: a fighting movement that is exactly as it sounds

Bain (m): an expert Neomeon healer

Bat: a small, black flying animal, allies with Black

Bat Tongue: a dragon disease that makes your tongue black and your throat dry

Beesting (m): yellow drah of the Third Age; part of the Killing of the Killer quest; later became a sofin trader; son of Sun and Honey; called Sting

Black (m): the fifth dragon to be created; best fighter of the original dragons (besides, possibly, Yellow); different from the others

Black Council: a meeting Black holds with all the bats and the purple tribe

Blood Feast: a rampage for blood by all vampire bats on the first day of autumn

Blue (m): the third dragon to be created, he loves water, prefers fish to eat, and has the best sense of humor of the original dragons; called Bat Defeater, Joke Maker, and Fish Eater

Bruoo (m): Darondo's servant; has a habit of calling Darondo "Your grace" which Darondo dislikes

Buffa-Day: a favorite holiday where all the Neomeons hunt buffalo and the Neomeon who catches the biggest gets to be a second king or queen for a day

Caios Neos: the name of the new tribe when the Lios Neos and the Caivat joined together

Caivat: Neomeons who were not against Black or with him, they simply wanted peace between the Lios Neos and the Svart Neos

Cave Bat: a lower bat to the vampire bats, live in caves

Cherryfly (f): mate to Rohawk; healer of the green tribe in the Second Age

Chill Orb: invented by white dragons, it looks like a silver metallic ball; when thrown at someone or something the air around it cools, and the person or object freeze; it is then controllable by voice;

Colo: See Melendi

Cloudhopper (m): purple drah, born in the Fourth Age; part of the purple dragon revolt

Crasila (f): Neomeon daughter of Diamond and Krengel

Crinjay (m): purple drah; battle dragon of the purple tribe in the Second Age

Crowhead: a field resembling a crow head near Sun Woods

Crunch (m): Neomeon member of the Svart Neos in the Fourth Age; one of Black's generals

Dangle (m): purple drah; hunter of the purple tribe during the Second Age; friend of Mistyeye; later proprietor of Dangle's Dragon Valley Antiques

Daraan (m): Neomeon king following Dairose, son of Zong

Dare (m): Neomeon king, Darondo's great grandson; joined with Black for an A+ sofin; the first leader of the Svart Neos

Darkroot (m): gray dragon in the Fourth Age who used to be yellow; as a draco he wandered into the wilderness, and his scales turned gray; became a great battle dragon and Yellow's general; trained battle dragon apprentices

Darnox (m): Neomeon king of the Caios Neos in the Fourth Age; almost died in the Battle of the Bones

Darondo (m): Neomeon king; he was very wise and strong and a friend of Yellow; nicknamed Dar, he died unexpectedly (most likely murdered)

Death Ceremony: a Neomeon ceremony, a burial

Dewong (m): Neomeon king; son of Diamond and Krengel, mate of Cadali

Diamond (f): a Neomeon, Darondo's daughter; nicknamed Di, she became queen after Darondo's death; best friend of Yellow, lived an extremely long life for a Neomeon

Dohonda (m): first Neomeon king, considered a god by the mountain lions; caught the biggest buffalo ever; invented The Test

Draco: baby dragon

Dragon: a creature resembling a dinosaur with wings

Dragon Apprentice Training: a school (invented in the Third Age) for teaching young dragons various roles; each dragon chooses a job and becomes an apprentice; eventually the apprentice will advance to his mentor's rank

Dragon Valley: the valley in which the dragons live

Drah: male dragon

Drai: female dragon

Dragonflies: a race of flying insects, enemies of the fireflies, allies of the dragons

Dragonfly Message Centers: yellow balls hanging from trees in the valley during the Fourth Age where dragonflies retrieve and send messages

Dream Cavern: temporary living place of the original dragons, named because they didn't dream the first night they found it

Dr. Ray T. Huffman Jr. (m) : a famous human inventor of the 2040's; created the five original dragons and trained them; called by the dragons Ray of Knowledge and Very Old Ray

Dugwe-quah (m): Neomeon king, son of Dewong and Cadali; called Dugwe

Evleen (f): a bat, Vron's mate

Fernpass (f): purple drai of the Third Age; daughter of Hugeflint and Min; part of the Killing of the Killer quest; became an expert battle dragon

Fireflies: a race of flying insects that can make their bottoms light up, enemies of the dragonflies

Fire Lake: a lake in Red's territory so named because the hot sun of the Desert makes it look as red as flame

Firestick: what dragons call a flashlight

Firestoper (m): red drah, born near the end of the Second Age; was a hunter and participant in the Tournament of Kings

Fish Heaven Lake: Blue's territory; largest lake of Dragon Valley, full of tasty fish

Flame (m): red drah of the third age, son of Rorwain; part of the Killing of the Killer quest and participant in the Tournament of Kings

Flipedge (m): father of Rorwain; battle dragon of the red tribe in the Second Age

Foosila (f): Neomeon daughter of Diamond and Krengel

Frogleap (m): green drah, mate of Mistyeye; a sofin trader who later became a knower; invented The Tournament of Kings in the Second Age; became the Head Shazar

Frostbeetle (m): white drah, born at the end of the Second Age; sofin trader and son of Whitelizard; participated in the Tournament of Kings

Gast (f): a so-called illusionist, but really a poison runekeeper

Gatheven (m): eldest son of Vron the vampire bat; nicknamed Gathe

Gleam (m): see Rage

Glix (m): raccoon, father of Nix; an extremely experienced smith and poet who declared, "You'll never have a good rating if you don't have plating," and "The beating of a hammer is the best kind of glamour."

Goldentree (f): yellow drai, born in the beginning of the Second Age; a knower and participant in the Tournament of Kings

Gongplain (m): prince of green tribe during the Second Age

Goose Lake: large lake near Dragon Valley

Gopherhill (M): red drah; captain of the sofin traders and a sofin grader

Gorcaak (m): king of the fireflies in the Fourth Age; he died in the Battle of the Bones

Gorn (m): a bat, Black's servant

Grabbing Trees: trees on Shadow Island that supposedly grab flying animals out of the air

Green (f): the first second generation dragon and first green dragon, daughter of Blue and Yellow; when older, she gained the territory west of Black's

Grend (m): Neomeon, father of Jelna and son of Foosila

Grit (m): a Slitherer, Sargoth's second in command

Grizz: bears

Grizzclaw: dragon-bears, bears with bat-like purple wings who prefer to avoid conflict

Grub (m): a fat, old Slitherer, who runs Grub's Grub

Grub's Grub: a Slitherer tavern, which serves grubs and is adjacent to jail cells

Grunn (f): a snake, friend of Nix, very nagging

Hazelblossom (f): a green drai of the Third Age, daughter of Rohawk; she later became a princess

Healer: a dragon who heals

Honey (f): yellow drai princess, born in the Second Age

Hootie: an owl

Hugeflint (m): purple drah, father of Fernpass and prince of the purple tribe in the Second Age; one of Black's advisors, he participated in the Tournament of Kings

Hultark (m): dragonfly of the Fourth Age, son of King Larwar; he became king when his father died in the Battle of the Bones

Hunter: hunts for dragon tribe

Huskoasion (m): very strong red drah, ally of Black, Gast's partner

Jash: a fighting movement, standing on your back claws then jumping and slashing in the air

Jelna (f): Neomeon daughter of Grend and best friend to Green

Jester Mountebank (m): green dragonfly; early in his life he was a bard in Patroesamenea; he then became a green dragonfly captain and part of the Killing of the Killer quest

Jolly Ringer: Raccoons who travel the valley looking for jobs to do in return for payment (also known as Pollyhemus Hirajae in raccoon tongue). Nix was the most famous of the group.

King Luthain Twi Gwamba the 31st (M): king of dragonflies in the First Age

Knower: a job created at the beginning of the Third Age; keeps track of (and makes sure everyone remembers) Dragon Valley's history

Kodge: a fighting movement, dodging and then kicking your opponent

Koik (m): Neomeon of the Caivat in the Second Age

Krengel (m): Diamond's mate, king of Neomeons in the First Age

Kunaash (m): a firefly captain in the Second Age

Larwar (m): king of the dragonflies in the Fourth Age; died in the Battle of the Bones

Leader: a term meaning the leader of a territory

Lilypath (f): blue drai, born in the Second Age, was a healer and mother of Rifttaker

Lios Neos (Light Neomeons): Neomeons who refused to join Black, they re-settled in Mount Leo

Madame Fang (f): see Poisonfang

Magic: something the dragons never quite understood, see runekeeper

Maple (f): a purple drai, born in the Fourth Age; one of the leaders of the purple dragon revolt

Meeting of Ray: a meeting the original dragons (and Green and Purple) held each month to discuss events and solve problems

Melendi (f): a Neomeon, an extremely good hunter, who was very kind to Darondo; once won Buffa-Day and named her buffalo Colo; she was temporary queen until Diamond was old enough

Merellia (f): a Caivat Neomeon, she didn't leave her tribe until she was part of the Killing of the Killer quest; later became the symbol of hope among the Neomeons

Min (f): purple drai, mother of Fernpass and healer of the purple tribe in the Second Age; good-hearted hated by every purple dragon but Mistyeye

Mirtlern (m): a cave bat supposedly killed by grabbing trees; he is a bat myth

Mistyeye (f): purple drai, best friend and later mate of Frogleap; sofin balancer; she rebelled against Black; had a scar running from her snout to her tail; the first dragon to turn gray

Moon Cave: Black's cave on Shadow Island

Mormus (m): blue drah, born in the Second Age; was a great hunter and participated in the Tournament of Kings

Mountain Lion: see Neomeon

Mull (m): Neomeon of the Caivat during the Second Age

Nix (m): a racoon, son of Glix; skilled in singing and smithing; he once made armor for the original dragons (and Green) to fight off bats

Neomeons: mountain lions who lived in the southeast of the valley in three mountains - Mount Leo, Echo Mountain, and Aexis Peak; they are very noble and have rulers called kings and queens; in the Second Age, they divided into three tribes; by the Fourth Age, they were two tribes

Pait: a fighting movement, where an opponent jumps at you and you hold out a claw for them to fall into

Patroesamenea: palace of the dragonflies

Petalswim (f): blue drai, born in the Fourth Age; her father was a battle dragon

Pink (f): what Purple should have been

Poisonfang (f): a bat of the Fourth Age; one of Black's generals and one of his best fighters; killed by Yellow

Pokewing (m): a bat of the Fourth Age, one of Black's generals

Prince or princess: second in command behind the leader of tribe

Prince Argvast Gwamba (m): the first dragonfly to meet the dragons; a great leader, son of King Luthain

Puddlejump (f): green drai, daughter of Frogleap and Mistyeye; later became a sofin trader

Purple (f): first purple dragon, daughter of White and Red; Black's longtime ally

Rage (m): red drah, son of Rorwain; his real name is Gleam but he calls himself Rage; participated in the Tournament of Kings

Rastlen (m): Neomeon of the Caios Neos during the Fourth Age; King Darnox's general

Rattlesler: a rattlesnake

Ray's glasses: Ray lost them near the beginning of the First Age; they were found by Slitherers in the Third Age; a holy object in the eyes of the dragons

Realflazing: a ball of fire that red dragons can create; can destroy anything but another fire ball

Red (f): the first dragon to be created; also the first dragon to fly; mate of White; also called Fast Wing, Desert Dweller, and Sheep Stalker

Rifttaker (m): blue drah of the Third Age, son of Riverpace and Lilypath; part of the Killing of the Killer quest; later became a great fish hunter; called Rift

Riverpace (m): blue drah, born in the Second Age; battle dragon and father of Rifttaker

Rohawk (m): hunter of the green tribe during the Second Age; was bitten by a rattlesler at age 17 and was never the same; could not sleep well, so his eyes turned red; killed in the Second Age

Rorwain (m): red drah; had to cross Black's territory when grizz separated him from his tribe; later accused of murder

Rulebender (m): Grizzclaw of the Fourth Age, who (unlike the other Grizzclaw) disliked solitude and neutrality; son of Swiftwing

Runekeeper: a dragon who uses runes of magic

Runekeeper Keep: a fort founded by Treepalm and Sundrop in Green's territory

Sargoth the Small (m): leader of Slitherers in the Fourth Age; the Dragon Valley magic didn't affect him properly, so he didn't grow; small but smart; attacks by slashing at ankles

Scaletail: a fish

Sevrem (m): large yellow drah born in the Second Age; a hunter who participated in the Tournament of Kings

Shadow Island: an island in Fish Heaven Lake, part of Black's territory; location of the Grabbing Trees

Shimmer (m): green drah of the Fourth Age, a runekeeper

Sler: a snake

Slitherers: a race of giant snakes; they are bandits, rogues, outcasts, assassins, and spies; they live in the northwest of Dragon Valley

Snoweye (f): white drai, born near the end of the Second Age; a healer who participated in the Tournament of Kings

Sofin: a comfortable moss, used to trade to the Neomeons for food, supplies, and help

Sofin Trader: There are three groups in sofin trading - the sofin finder, sofin grader, and sofin balancer. The sofin finder finds the sofin and gives it to the sofin graders who grade the sofin A, B, or C (or occasionally the rare, pure white A+ sofin). Sofin balancers provide the right amount of sofin to the Neomeons for food, supplies, and assistance.

Spalgrin (m): blue drah, born near the end of the Second Age; a prince who participated in the Tournament of Kings

Sparklight (f): red drai, born in the Second Age; Rorwain's mate

Splash (m): blue drah, born in the Fourth Age; Blue's general

Springseeker (f): green drai, born in the Fourth Age; one of the head dragons in Runekeeper Keep; 37th great-granddaughter of Treepalm

Steamsnort (m): purple drah, born in the Fourth Age; second in command to Twig and Maple among the rebels; very clumsy

Sterlingflower (f): green drai in the Third Age, daughter of Rohawk; later became a hunter

Stormglaze (m): blue drah, born near the end of the Second Age; a battle dragon who participated in the Tounament of Kings

Streakedegg (m): green drah; battle dragon of the Second Age who participated in the Tournament of Kings

Stump (m): yellow drah, born in the Second Age; a Battle Shazar and healer in the Third Age

Sun (m): yellow drah, born in the Second Age; hunter and father of Beesting

Sundrop (m): yellow drah, born in the Second Age; a sun runekeeper who helped Treepalm and his friends escape the Slitherers; founded Runekeeper Keep with Treepalm

Svart Neos (Dark Neomeons): Neomeons who joined Black in his quest for power, re-settled in Echo Mountain

Swiftwing (m): leader of the Grizzclaw in the Fourth Age; called Swiftwing because of his fast wings

Swishy Creek: The largest river in the valley, running northeast from Fish Heaven Lake.

Syonim: a food invented by white dragons; it is frozen sap that tastes sweet and makes your body feel warm

Tailtinge (f): red drai, born in the Fourth Age; a young knower

Territory: a region of land that a dragon or other creature calls home

The Box: a box Black discovered, which was labelled: Magic

The Split Kingdom: the three Neomeon kingdoms, the Lios Neos, Svart Neos, and Caivat

The Test: a test for a Neomeon to become king or queen; except for the fact that your mother must name you starting with the letter D, the test is really nothing, which must be kept a secret

Tinwain (f): red drai, mother of Rorwain and hunter in the Second Age

Tournament of Kings: a contest between members of various dragon tribes; a Head Shazar selects the top five dragons, and a specific Shazar for each tournament chooses the five worst

Treeboard: a sort of whiteboard for dragons on the side of a tree

Treepalm (m): great green drah of the Third Age, son of Rohawk; part of the Killing of the Killer quest; later became a knower and runekeeper and founded Runekeeper Keep

Twig (m): purple drah, born in the Fourth Age; one of the leaders of the purple rebellion

Tuddthromius (m): a Neomeon of the Caivat in the Second Age; called Tudd

Vampire Bat: a blood-sucking bat

Vilton (m): youngest son of Vron the vampire bat; called Vil

Vine Mountebank (m): a green dragonfly of the Fourth Age; the 1,542nd great-grandson of Jester Mountebank; killed by Black

Vron (m): a vampire bat, best friend of Black; has an odd accent, even for bats

War of Conquest: the third war of the Split Kingdom

Wingsweep (f): gray drai, daughter of Frogleap and Mistyeye; later became a hunter and gray like her mother

White (m): the fourth dragon to be created, the shyest and most secretive of the original dragons; loves the cold

Whitelizard (m): white drah, born in the Second Age; was a knower and part of the Killing of the Killer quest; father of Frostbeetle

Whitelizard the 28th (m): white drah, leader of white dragons in the Fourth Age

Xiana: a long horn of sorts (invented by Green) that can be placed in the crack of a boulder or tree branch; it was used to speak with other dragon leaders through sound

Xillar (m): a Neomeon of the Caios during the Fourth Age; chief Neomeon storyteller

Yellow (f): the second dragon to be created; a friend to Neomeons, her nickname was Yellie; the bravest and best fighter of the original dragons (besides, possibly, Black); called Sofin Trader, Neomeon Friend, Rabbit Hunter, and Problem Solver

Zong (m): Neomeon, father of Daraan

ABOUT THE AUTHOR

Luke Herzog began writing *Dragon Valley* at the age of nine and completed it the day before his eleventh birthday. He lives with his parents, his brother and his dog, Pippin, on California's Monterey Peninsula. His favorite authors include Christopher Paolini, DJ MacHale and J.R.R. Tolkien. This is his first published novel. Currently he is working on his next novel, a fantasy adventure about a good-hearted rogue named Griffin Blade. Explore more of Dragon Valley at www.dragon-valley.com.

Made in the USA
Lexington, KY
21 April 2012